# FOOL ME ONCE

NICOLE WILLIAMS

*For the Reality Heroines.*

# 1

SOME THINGS WEREN'T MEANT TO BE. THAT'S what I told myself for the thousandth time when I caught sight of my ex with his newest flame.

"You're too good for him."

"*Way* too good for him."

My childhood friends, Brooke and Sophia, assured me as they circled in tighter.

"I don't know why I decided to come to this thing," I muttered before finishing what was left in my champagne glass.

"Maybe because a ten-year high school reunion only happens once in a lifetime?" Brooke spun me around so the happy couple wasn't in view, while Sophia dashed off to grab another glass of champagne.

"You know what? A hysterectomy is a once-in-a-lifetime kind of thing too, but I'm not going to sign myself up just because." I checked the time, my shoulders falling when I did. Barely an hour in and I already felt like this experience had extinguished whatever patience was left in my person.

"Just be thankful you didn't waste any more time on a guy like that. Chalk it up to experience and move on."

"And look at the line of men I have to move on with?" I motioned at the area in front of me; it was empty. "I should have been smart like you and Sophia and gotten married young to some nice, hard-working local boy."

"Would you stop? You're twenty-eight. It's not like you're horizontal and decaying," Brooke put her hand on her hip, leveling me with a serious look.

"No. I'm decaying vertically"—I tapped the corners of my eyes, where I'd detected the early stages of crow's feet earlier this summer—"practicing for my future as a cranky old spinster."

"You girls talking about me behind my back again?" Sophia reappeared with a fresh glass of champagne, practically ramming it into my hand.

"Please. We prefer to direct our insults to your face." I winked at Sophia as we clinked our glasses.

"That's a sign of true friendship," Brooke toasted before we all took a drink.

"Hey, ladies, this isn't homeroom. Break it up and dance already." Rob, Brooke's husband, popped up beside us, ringing his arm around his wife's neck.

"I hate this song." My nose curled as I stayed planted in place.

The three of them headed toward the dance floor as Sophia made a face at me and said, "It was eleven years ago. Time to let it go, girl."

Brady, her husband, joined her for a dance.

"Not likely," I said under my breath, taking in the party from my spectator seat on the sidelines.

Almost everyone had made their way to the dance floor, singing at the tops of their lungs. I didn't know how anyone could stand to hear this song after it had been played nonstop on the radio the past four months.

Jesse, another of my good friends, settled beside me. "Do you think he's going to show?"

"There aren't any cameras or fancy awards, so unlikely," I grumbled.

"Ever since the accident, it seems like he's been

keeping a low profile anyway." Jesse waved the bird at my ex, who was too busy lodging his tongue down his dance partner's throat to notice. "I still can't believe Chase was that drunk. I mean, blowing a point two isn't for the faint of heart, and I don't remember him drinking at a party even once when the rest of us were being rebellious teenagers."

I rolled my eyes at my friend, who had this concerned expression as though Chase was the victim. "There was also the bit about him plowing his truck into a parked car and getting arrested."

"Fame and money really ruin people." Jesse clucked her tongue. "That's why I'm so grateful to live paycheck to paycheck and have good friends who babysit for free at the drop of a hat." Jesse nudged me. "Thank you again for last night. Johnny and I had a really nice night. Adult conversation, dinner that wasn't some variation of mac n' cheese, and I got to wear earrings without fear of having them ripped out by grabby baby hands."

"They were perfect angels for me, as always." I smiled at her. "And you're welcome. Any time."

"How are you?" Before I could even attempt to give the bullshit answer, Jesse added, "For real?"

"I'm okay. Learning to accept I might be happier alone than the alternative." My eyes had wandered to a certain couple moving in such a way that made clothes seem pointless.

"You haven't met the right one."

"Because the right one isn't out there." I wound my arm around hers, hoping that would be the end of the conversation.

My friends cared, and that's why they felt the need to dissect my every relationship-gone-wrong, but the last thing I wanted to do was detail my failures in the romance department. Especially with three friends who were happily married and starting their own families.

"Of course he's out there. You can't give up hope."

I lifted my glass. "In my fourteen years of dating, I've been cheated on, lied to, broken up with over a social media messenger, heartbroken, ditched for an eight-figure record deal, and proposed to by seven African princes." My gaze dropped to my bare left ring finger. "I have just enough hope left to say yes to the next prince who asks for my hand."

Jesse shook her head. "He's out there. And when you agree to marry him, it better be me you call to be your maid of honor."

"Deal." I clinked my nearly empty glass to hers,

which was already empty. "Whatcha drinking? My treat for the relationship counseling."

"A screwdriver." She handed me her glass. "Hold the alcohol."

"Wait. What?" It took me two seconds of confusion before my eyes dropped to her stomach. "Number three?"

Jesse's hand lowered to her stomach. "All four and a half months of him or her."

My face lit up before I threw myself at her, winding my arms around her as much as I could with two glasses in my hands. "Congratulations! I'm so happy for you guys."

"Thanks, friend. I don't know what I'm going to do with three in diapers, but I guess I'll figure it out."

"Are you kidding? You'll more than figure it out. You are, like, the best mom ever." I planted a kiss on her cheek before backing toward the bar. "I'm going to get some drinks to celebrate. Virgin screwdrivers coming right up."

Jesse flashed a rock and roll symbol, biting her tongue. I chuckled before turning around so I didn't run into someone or something. With the three glasses of champagne I had in my all of five-foot-four frame, it was an Easter miracle I was still upright.

I'd just made it to the bar when a chorus of cheers reverberated through the room. Jason Gallagher had probably stripped to his skivvies and was doing the moonwalk like he used to do every last day of school from the time we hit middle school.

But then I heard a familiar name being called out, practically chanted.

Good god, no. My luck wasn't that bad.

Oh, wait.

Setting the empty glasses on the counter, I slowly turned around, praying I was mishearing the name still ringing through the reception room.

I saw him right away, as though my eyes were trained to find him in a crowded room. I hated that they still followed that habit.

There he was, Chase Lawson, the legend himself, sauntering into a high school reunion in the same small town he'd waved farewell to eleven years ago.

My stomach knotted as I scanned the nearest exits.

"What can I get you?" The bartender interrupted my mini panic attack.

"Um . . ." I tried to remember a simple drink order. It was difficult with two ex flames in the same crowded room. "Two screwdrivers." I fumbled with the bills inside my leather clutch. "Two *virgin* screwdrivers." I remembered right as he was about to pour in the vodka.

"So two orange juices?" He gave me a look that suggested I was even more unhinged than I thought. He shook his head when I held out a twenty. "On the house."

"Thanks."

I grabbed my OJs and hugged the perimeter as I made my way back to where I'd left Jesse. Except she'd been pulled onto the dance floor by her husband and was way too close to Chase and his ever-present following of fawning females for my comfort. Making a last-minute decision, I ducked through the half-open door leading outside.

"I knew I shouldn't have come," I said to myself before taking a sip of one of the orange juices. It wasn't like I'd had to travel or rent a hotel—Jericho High was a whole four miles from my family's farm —but I doubted I'd feel more inconvenienced if they'd held it on some iceberg in the Arctic.

Following the walkway toward the small pond tucked behind the reception hall, I settled onto the first bench I came across. My feet were killing me thanks to the weapons of torture I'd selected for tonight. My feet were used to boots, not four-inch strappy heels. But according to Sophia, our town's resident fashion maven, the royal blue heels were exactly what my scarlet cocktail dress was in need of. We'd all felt really high class rolling into Tulsa a couple weekends ago to hit the mall for our reunion digs, but some articles were better suited for hangers than bodies. Mine in particular. I'd never in my life had to work so hard to take a full breath.

Once I'd torn off the shoes I had plans to drop off at Goodwill tomorrow, I sat back, made my best attempt at relaxing, and stared at the sky. It was overcast, but a few stars were popping through the thick clouds. How many times had I stared at that sky as a young woman, spinning plans that would never come to fruition? Dreaming dreams that would never connect with reality?

Too damn many, that's the closest I could get.

I'd had plans to travel, to visit every continent before I had kids, and I'd barely made it to a handful of bordering states since. The upside was that I wasn't going to be a mother anytime soon, if ever, so I still had plenty of time to visit those continents.

"Is this where the Anti-Social Club meets?"

I flinched so hard, I wound up with the majority of two cups of juice on my lap. Add the dress to the Goodwill pile. "Turn around. Go away."

A low-timbered chuckle. "You always had a way with words, Em."

My head whipped over my shoulder. "Uh-oh. No. You do not get to call me Em."

Chase flashed one of his infamous smiles, the one that had made him a hit with the ladies before his face had been plastered across billboards, magazines, and screensavers. It was the part-smirk, mostly-smolder grin. Right dimple set. Cobalt eyes flashing. What Celebrity Instagrammers had labeled the underwear-incinerator.

But not these underwear. Chase Lawson had no sway over the condition of my underwear anymore.

"Okay, *Emma*." The sound of Chase's boots connecting with the pavement made my teeth grind together. In a different life, I'd loved the sound of his boots as he moved closer. "Is this seat taken?"

"Yes." I slammed the empty glasses on the bench, lifting my eyebrow at him.

"Sorry about the dress," he said when his eyes dipped to the wet circles dotting my stomach.

"Of all the things to apologize for, my dress is not high on the list."

His smile stretched. "I've missed having someone around whose primary language isn't bullshit."

"Is that meant as a compliment?"

"Obviously."

Inhaling, I twisted in my seat so my back was angled toward him. No matter how many pieces of confetti Chase Lawson had diced my heart into when he left me, it wasn't safe for any red-blooded woman to stare at him face-on at this close of a distance. Not unless she was in the market for a heartbreak.

"How have you been, Em—Emma?" He caught himself, but from his smirk, the slip had probably been intentional.

"Amazing." I breathed through my mouth when a familiar scent hit my senses. I couldn't believe he still wore the same cologne. It seemed like I should have had some kind of proprietary right over it since I was the one who got it for him on our first Christmas together.

"How amazing?"

"Amazingly amazing." When I caught him

glancing at my left hand, I tucked my hands beneath my legs.

"Good to hear."

I bit my cheek, wondering if I could figure out a way to time travel to freshman year when I'd agreed to be Chase Lawson's date to homecoming. Even the fourteen-year-old version of me had known getting involved with Chase was equivalent to playing a game of Russian Roulette. She hadn't heeded the warning, but she'd at least acknowledged it.

"If you're looking for your fans, you'll find them back in there." My thumb hitched over my shoulder. "I know you can't go more than a few minutes without being worshipped or else you risk spontaneous combustion."

"Please. I can go a good ten minutes without being worshipped now. I've matured." I heard the smile in his voice, but damned if I was going to check for it. That was the one-hundred percent smirk one.

"What are you doing out here?" I asked. "We both know you're the center-of-the-crowd type, not the wallflower who sneaks off to be alone."

From the corner of my eyes, I saw him slip his hands into the pockets of his snug jeans. Another

Chase Dawson trademark—close-fitting jeans to better emphasize an agreeable rear and an even more agreeable swell around front.

"A person can change," he said, his shoulders lifting. "A person *does* change when all day, every day they're surrounded by people and noise."

My eyes lifted. "Must be difficult making all of that money from all of those adoring fans."

"I'm not going to be able to say anything without you twisting it, am I?"

A wave of exhaustion came over me as though twenty-eight years of life had decided to catch up to me all at once. "I don't want to fight with you."

"Could have fooled me."

I chipped away at the fresh pale pink polish on my nails, a nervous habit. It was the first manicure I'd had in years, and it hadn't survived twelve hours. "Why did you come back?"

His head tipped toward the reception hall. "It was the ten-year reunion."

A huff escaped from my mouth. "Please, you left this place and haven't so much as spared a second thought for anything or anyone here. And some lame reunion in the Best Western ballroom is the can't miss event of the summer?"

He rubbed the back of his neck in a familiar

way. Used as a stalling measure when he was trying to figure out what to say and how to say it, it was a display I was all too acquainted with.

"I came back from one reason." He slowly angled in my direction. When he let out a breath, his gaze all-intentional, my chest seized.

"Me?" I screeched, at the same time choking on a laugh. "You're out of your damn mind if you think I've been waiting here, on pins and needles, for you. Keep on strutting back to that fancy Nashville estate of yours, because the only part of you I still want is the cautionary tale."

Chase's hand rubbed his jaw, his smile unmistakable despite his efforts to erase it. "I didn't come back for you," he stated, promptly bringing a flush to my face.

Of course he wasn't there for me. The seventeen-year-old version hadn't expressed any qualms ditching me as an up-and-comer; the twenty-eight-year-old country icon certainly wasn't back to rekindle anything.

"Sorry to burst your bubble, even though I can tell you'll be all torn up knowing that," he said.

"Good to hear you still have a knack for sarcasm."

He crouched beside the bench, staring at the

dark pond. I was more concerned with checking the shrubs and shadows for any signs of the paparazzi he seemed to attract wherever he went. Literally, everywhere. Some dude had managed to snap a picture of Chase through his Tennessee estate's bathroom window, fresh from the shower and shaving. The thirst for Chase Lawson had gone from parched to panting in one intimate image.

"I've got a new album that just dropped," he said. "A whirlwind tour kicking off next week. I've had a bit of a public image problem this past year, and my PR team assured me that getting back to my roots will help shift that."

My fingers snapped. "I knew this had something to do with the media. By the way, where is the camera squad tonight?"

"Somewhere. They're always around."

"I'm sure you really hate all that attention," I chided, wondering how much more I had to throw at him before he'd move on.

"I came back because I need to clean up my image and do some damage repair to my reputation." He went back to rubbing the back of his neck. "Now that I'm here with you, and you sort of accused me of being here for you, a crazy idea popped to mind."

"I'd like to recommend you keep this idea to yourself," I suggested, but he was already talking.

"If I had my old high school girlfriend with me on tour—rekindling an old flame with a small-town country girl—how could that not clean up an image?" He motioned at me. "You're exactly what I need to show fans I'm getting my life back on track. A wholesome, down-to-earth girl who gets up at five to water the horses instead of going to bed at that hour after drinking the town dry."

My head whipped in his direction, finally looking at him to determine if he was being serious. My god, he was.

"Not a chance in hell," I said, enunciating each word slowly.

Chase didn't blink. "Even if that proposition was tied to a sum of money?" When I opened my mouth to argue, he added, "A *large* sum?"

"My principles aren't for sale."

He shuffled a little closer, still kneeling. Damn. He was just as attractive in person from three feet away as he was on the cover of *Rolling Stone*. My stomach knotted again, but this time for a different reason.

"I don't want to buy your principles." One brow lifted. "Just six months of your time."

For a minute, I sat there silently, part hypnotized by his presence, part contemplating his ridiculous offer. There were few people I disliked more than Chase Lawson, but I also had big plans for my future. Plans that necessitated money.

"How much?"

My head shook when I heard my question out loud. What was I saying? What was I actually contemplating doing?

"One hundred thousand a month," he replied.

My hand curled around the arm of the bench. "Six hundred thousand dollars?" I shrieked, giving him a look like he was crazy.

"Fine. Six months. One million dollars." He exhaled. "Final offer."

My hand was dangerously close to ripping the handle from the bench. "One million dollars."

My mind raced with everything I could do with that money. Restoring the farmhouse the way I'd dreamed, turning it into a quaint B&B with an agrarian twist. Spoiling my parents with a fancy cruise and a new farm truck. *Finally* getting to travel to some of the places I'd only imagined through the pictures of a magazine.

All it would take was six months with Chase.

It wasn't exactly an easy decision, but it wasn't a

hard one. I'd given two years of my life to him already, and it had cost me more than I'd been prepared to pay. This time, he'd be the one paying for it. One million dollars to be exact.

I couldn't answer quickly enough. "Deal."

**2**

"Are you sure you know what you're doing?"
My mom glanced across the stable at me.

"I'm positive," I replied, hoping my answer
sounded more convincing than I felt on the matter
of spending the next half a year with Chase.

"You wanted to burn the man at the stake
yesterday and this morning you're leaving with him
to pose as his girlfriend?"

I focused on mucking out the stalls instead of
meeting my mom's all-penetrating stare. She could
see a lie coming from me before I'd even conceived
it. "I'm doing it for the million bucks. That's all."

"And I wouldn't have thought you'd do it for a
billion with the way he left you." She grunted,
muttering something under her breath. My parents

weren't what you'd consider big fans of Chase Lawson—the star or the man. "What are you going to tell all of your friends?"

"Well, I can't tell them about Chase's and my agreement like I told you and Dad. The whole point of this thing is for everyone to think the perfect Chase Lawson reunited with his high school sweetheart after getting sober and putting his life back on track. If anyone found out he was paying for me to pretend . . ." I set the pitchfork aside to lay some fresh straw. "Pretty sure that would do the opposite of shining up his reputation like he's hoping for."

"It's not like Chase ever had a decent reputation to being with. Why's he so concerned about it now?" Mom moved down to the next stall.

Both of us were moving quicker than normal since a car would be coming for me soon.

"Don't know. Don't care. I'm just in it for the money."

"As your mother, half of me winces when I hear my daughter agreed to pose as a man's lover, and half of me is proud of her for being so industrious."

I chuckled as I spread the hay. "Same goes for me exactly."

"But really, honey, you're going to have to tell

your friends something. Soon. Before they hear it in the tabloids and start a petition to have you involuntarily committed."

"I know. I will." I took a deep breath once I'd finished the stall. Morning chores were officially done—and in record time too. "I'll call Jesse and tell her some story about Chase and I reconnecting the night of the reunion and that I'm going to, for once in my life, be reckless. I'll ask her to spread the word to the others, then when I return in six months, fresh from a breakup, they'll get back to trying to set me up with anyone under the age of sixty who isn't married."

Mom came up beside me, tugging off her leather work gloves. "Sounds like you've got it all planned out."

"At least some of it," I said, ringing my arm around her as we left the barn.

I'd miss this place. A lot. I'd miss the morning and evening chores, the smell of the air after a light summer rain, and the sounds of farm animals bringing in twilight. I'd miss my little apartment, meeting for Saturday night BBQs, and swimming in the creek outside of town.

I loved this small patch of earth where time moved slower and people cared about the strength of their relationships more than the balance in their bank account. It was because I loved this place so much that I was leaving. I'd be back. Seven figures richer.

"You know, you could always get a loan from the bank to get the money you need to renovate the old farmhouse." Mom's chin lifted in the direction of the house built by my great-great grandfather in the 1870s. It hadn't been lived in for decades, and even though it looked like the setting of a potential horror film right now, new paint, windows, and a loving touch would change the whole image.

"I could, but my grandkids would still be repaying it. This way, I don't have to repay anyone."

Mom made a face. "But you have to give up six months of your life to that man."

"Who said achieving your dreams was going to be easy?" I bumped my hip against hers as we headed toward where Dad was finishing refilling the watering troughs.

"Fine. Point taken. Just . . . be careful."

"Promise."

Dad must have overheard our conversation because he pointed at me. "That boy hurts you again, Em, and it won't matter how much reasoning you or your mama throw at me, he's going to be picking my shotgun shells out of his hind end for weeks." Dad grunted, shaking his head as he closed the livestock gate behind him. "He'd write a song about it no doubt. Capitalize on getting shot by the father of his ex-girlfriend. Title it, 'Break Her Heart, Get Shot in the Ass.'"

Mom and I laughed.

"It would probably be a number-one hit too," Mom teased.

The sound of a car crunching up the long driveway caught our attention. They were early.

"It's not too late to back out." Dad nudged me before waving at the pasture where the horses were. "Old Sonny can outrun that big, shiny tank."

"Not backing out." I loped toward the small house the limo was stopping in front of. There wasn't a place within fifty miles where a person could rent a limo, so they must have gotten someone to come all the way out here from Tulsa.

The driver was already opening the back passenger door by the time I made it over. A petite blond woman in a smart black suit popped out of the backseat, staring at the house as though it were contaminated. My grandparents had had this smaller home built after the original farmhouse became uninhabitable without some significant repairs, and this was where my parents had brought me home from the hospital. I didn't like some big city woman giving it the stink-eye.

"Morning!" I called, waving to get her attention.

"You're Emma?" When the woman's attention diverted to me, her stare at the house had seemed warm by comparison.

I flicked the bill of my hat. "That's me."

Her eyes wandered down me, a deep line carving between her brows when they fell on my boots. "I'm Dani, Chase's PA." Her throat cleared, her eyes still fixated on my boots. "Do you need any help with your bags?"

"I've only got one, so I think I can manage." I jogged up the porch steps and retrieved my suitcase from where it was resting beside the porch swing. "Is Chase in there?"

"He'll be waiting for us on the airplane."

"Smarter than he looks," I said, winking at my dad, who'd made his way with Mom toward the limo.

"What's that?" Dani asked, her tone as pleasant as her survey of me had been.

"Just an inside joke between my dad and me. And his shotgun."

Dad took my suitcase and loaded it into the trunk of the limo despite the driver offering to do it.

I felt tears wading to the surface, so I had to make the goodbye quick. It wasn't like I was leaving forever or wouldn't be able to call them whenever I wanted. But still. It was the longest I'd been away from the farm and this town ever.

After giving each of my parents a long, suffocating hug, I took a deep breath and climbed inside the limo. Dani was already waiting inside.

"Oh. I thought you might want to change first." She scooted farther down the seat.

"Why? Are we going straight to some fancy event or something?"

Chase hadn't gone into a ton of detail about what the six months would fully entail, but I knew appearances, dates, charity events, and a couple of awards shows were part of the job.

"No, we're just getting on an airplane. A private, luxury G-6 with ivory interior." She was back to staring at my boots.

"Chase grew up country too. He's no stranger to muddying up boots."

Dani pursed her lips. "No, but he doesn't typically traipse around with cow shit on his boots in public."

"Probably because the only cow he comes in contact with is the filet on his dinner plate," I muttered, inspecting my boots again. They really weren't that bad. But for a girl whose heels were so shiny she could see her reflection in them, I guessed my boots were a rural crime scene.

The driver had climbed inside, and I made sure to roll down the windows and wave at my parents as we headed down the driveway. The distraction kept me from saying something I'd regret to a person who I'd obviously spend a lot of the next six months around. She might not have liked me now because I had callouses on my palms and dirt under my nails, but she'd warm up to me eventually.

"Don't worry—this is more mud than it is manure. Two substances Chase has got to be used to after being in the public eye for a decade."

Dani was quiet for a few minutes, tapping around on her tablet like she had a thousand-item checklist to complete before nine o'clock. "So you two were really together? High school sweethearts?"

"For two years, yeah."

She made a sound with her mouth, still typing

away on the shiny tablet in her lap. "You seem like an unlikely pair."

I pulled at my old T-shirt, feeling a piece of straw stuck inside. "Unlikely. Disastrous. Volatile. Pick your adjective."

"Yet that didn't stop you from agreeing to fake as his girlfriend."

I took that as a rhetorical statement and left it at that. "You said you were his PA? What does that stand for?"

"Personal assistant," she replied, clearly not going to expand upon that unless pressed.

I pressed. "Well, you know, I'm a dumb hick who doesn't know their femur from their frontal lobe. What does being a PA entail?"

She cracked her window then rolled it back up when the wind blew through her flawlessly styled hair. "Personal. Assistance. In any and all capacities."

"Any and all?" I repeated.

"I'm basically his spouse, without the exchanging of vows." She looked up from her tablet, her brown eyes drilling into mine. "Does that clear things up?"

"Completely," I mouthed, wondering if there was a clinical term for someone who'd had a stick shoved so far up their butt they'd become poisoned by it.

We rode in silence until the small airfield outside of town came into view. A person usually never saw anything fancier than a crop duster or, every once in a while, a private single engine, but today was different. Chase's jet dwarfed the others dotted around the airstrip, gleaming in the early morning sun.

"The last private jet I was on was nicer, but this is acceptable."

Dani either didn't get my sense of humor or have one at all.

The instant the limo came to a stop, she was out the door, her tablet tucked into her buttery leather briefcase. I crawled out the other door and heaved my suitcase out of the trunk before the driver had made it out of his seat.

"Thanks for the ride." I waved at the driver before following Dani toward the plane, my old suitcase teetering like it was about to bust a wheel.

A woman in a navy suit similar to the one Dani had on took my suitcase at the base of the plane's stairway. Her smile was genuine though, and she even called me ma'am after saying good morning.

When I stepped inside the plane, I froze. I'd

flown a few times in my life, but coach class had nothing on a private jet. The fancy hotel I'd had lunch in with Mom in Oklahoma City didn't even boast the level of class found inside this flying tin cylinder.

I noticed him, rising from his seat, from the corner of my eye.

"The devil pays well," I greeted, making my way into the cabin.

I'd thought Dani was exaggerating about the ivory interior of the plane, but she wasn't.

"Yeah, well, my soul wasn't worth much to me, so it was an easy decision." Chase stepped out into the aisle, looking frustratingly gorgeous for this early in the morning. Here I was, ripe from early morning farm chores, and he looked as though he was freshly minted at the deity treasury.

I'd just started sliding out of my dirty boots when Chase interrupted. "Don't worry about it. I can't make it through a flight without spilling coffee or making some kind of mess, so my team's a bunch of pros when it comes to stain removal."

I went ahead and kicked off my boots anyways. If I'd tried stepping foot inside Mom's house with them on, I would have gotten what for. "My junior prom dress still bears the punch stains of your grace impairment."

His brow cocked. "*Just* the punch stains?"

I made it a point of staring at Dani, who was getting herself settled into one of the back seats, a laptop joining her tablet on the table in front of her.

He broke the silence with an amused grunt. "I was referring to the hot sauce stains from the order of wings we got after the dance and took out to the creek. What were you thinking about, perv?"

"Did you seriously call me a perv? So much for maturing."

A low-timbered chuckle echoed in his chest, his gaze unapologetic as I wound down the aisle. A corner of his mouth lifted when his inspection ended on my messy ponytail, my old farm supply hat resting low on my head. "You're a sight for these Oklahoma-roots eyes, Emma Young."

"Oh yeah. I'm sure you've missed the itch of straw falling inside your shirt and the scent of manure permanently embedded in your nostrils." I eyed his boots that looked fresh out of the box, right on up to his white tee that was so bright it was almost blinding.

"The straw and manure I definitely don't miss.

But those proud country girls who would just as soon shoot you as they would kiss you, I do miss."

One of my hands settled on my hip. "You don't have to tell lies in some attempt to woo me. This is a business transaction as far as I'm concerned."

He took his seat, indicating the empty one beside him. "I'm paying you seven figures. Don't think I'm stressing out trying to think of the right thing to say at the right time. If I tell you something, it's because I want to and it's the truth."

"Glad we got that cleared up." Settling into the plush seat beside him, I couldn't believe the difference between this plane seat and the ones I'd been in before. The chair was twice as wide, and it came with a recliner feature that leaned back so far a person could sleep if they wanted. There was even a massage button.

"Having fun?" Chase interrupted my fiddling with the chair, but not before I found the heated seat option.

"You are a true rags-to-riches story," I said, shaking my head in awe as the plane taxied.

"If only my old man could see me now." Chase grunted. "He'd probably still tell me I was a worthless piece of shit."

My teeth worked at my lip as I debated how to

respond. Chase's dad had been that in title alone, making your typical bad father seem like a candidate for parent of the year. "I heard he passed on a few years ago." I couldn't bring myself to express sorrow for that demon of a man's death.

"It was the most selfless thing he'd ever done."

As the plane was about to take off, Chase sighed when he saw my seatbelt unfastened. Leaning over, he secured the belt over my lap, cinching it so tightly a puff of air came from my mouth.

"You're not wearing yours," I noted, looking away when I realized I was staring at his lap. He was wearing a different pair of jeans than he had on last night, but they were just as snug, more highlighting rather than hinting at his package.

"So?" His shoulder lifted as the plane's wheels lifted.

"So why was it so important I have mine on?"

He didn't answer. Instead, his head inclined toward the window, staring at the small town we'd grown up in together as it faded into non-existence. "I wasn't sure you were going to show."

"That makes two of us."

A dark suit swished up beside me, her tablet in hand. "We'll be touching down in Nashville at 9:13. The driver will be ready and waiting, which will put us back at your place at 9:54. Providing there are no accidents on the interstate which, as of now"— Dani checked the tablet once more, her eyebrows pinching together—"it's clear. Your team will be there waiting in the conference room, ready to go over the final details of the tour. Would you like to have any special food or drink out besides the usual?"

Chase seemed to be in a trance as he stared at the white billows of clouds flashing by the window. "Anything special you want, Emma?"

It took me a second to realize he was talking to me—I was so used to him calling me Em that my given name rolling off his tongue so naturally caught me by surprise. I spurted the first thing that came to mind. "Cotton candy."

Chase's chest moved.

"It's a morning collaboration meeting. Not a county fair." When Chase turned his head, one look had Dani scribbling something on her tablet. "Cotton candy. Consider it done." She aimed a smile at Chase before rustling back to her seat.

"I don't think Dani's a fan," I said under my voice.

"She's not a fan of the arrangement. It's nothing personal."

Making my point, I twisted in my seat to wave at her. She issued a curt look before unleashing fury on her laptop's keys.

"Pretty sure a little bit of it is personal," I said to him.

"Maybe."

"Any way to win her over? Salted caramels? Favorite perfume?" I asked, knowing I'd be spending a lot of time around her. I wasn't thrilled at the forecast of icy stares and moody confrontations.

"Her client's getting ready to kick off one of the biggest tours in history. He's also looking to convince the public that he's cleaned up his act and is the same decent, slightly damaged country boy they fell in love with a decade ago." He exhaled. "And she just got thrown a curve that her client's faking a rekindled romance with an old flame in the thirteenth hour. Nothing short of creating a carbon copy of Dani by this afternoon will warm her up to your presence. Or mine at this point."

"You should pay that girl more."

Chase's elbow brushed against mine on the armrest. "Believe me, she is well compensated for putting up with my bullshit."

The stewardess approached, offering to get us

something to drink. We both ordered black coffee. While we waited for her to bring them, Chase's head turned toward me. He waited for me to look at him.

When my eyes met his, he said, "I'm sorry."

"For what?"

His Adam's apple moved. "For number one on the list of what I have to apologize to you for."

My chest squeezed as tears welled behind my eyes. An apology. Finally. It didn't change anything, but somehow, it seemed to fix whatever piece of me he'd broken. "It's okay," I said. "I've moved on."

His attention drifted out the window again. "I haven't."

**3**

---

"WHAT DO YOU THINK?" CHASE LEANED ACROSS the limo seat to stare out the same window I was gawking out.

"It's big," were the words that tumbled from my mouth.

"It also came with a dishwasher," he teased as the limo came to a stop in front of the monstrosity.

Chase opened the door, stepped out, and waited for Dani and me to climb out. As small of a gesture as it was, it made me happy to know some of the old Chase was still there—the one who could open his own car doors without the help of a driver.

Dani was halfway up the pristine walkway, and I was still gaping at the place as though I was standing in front of the great pyramids or the Sistine Chapel.

"It's just a house."

"It's big enough to fit our entire hometown comfortably," I responded. "How many people live here with you?"

Chase started up the walkway with me, cracking his neck. "Just me."

"One person needs all of this?" I caught myself blinking at the extensive water feature resting in the middle of the circular driveway.

"I don't *need* all of this. But I listened to the advice of my investment people when they suggested I put a good chunk of my money in real estate."

"Looks like you dumped it all in real estate."

His pause tipped me off. The folds in his forehead told the rest.

"How many places do you own?" I asked.

The corners of his eyes creased. "In *this* country?"

"I can't even," I muttered, pausing outside the front door to peel off my boots. "The boy who used to dig for nickels in the couch cushions is richer than god now."

He waited with me, watching me wrestle with

my boots with an intense gleam in his eyes. "There's more to being rich than money."

"Says everyone who's got a bunch of it."

Padding inside the massive double doors that felt twice my height, I struggled to keep my eyeballs in their sockets. Everything had this shiny glow, from the tile floors to the paintings on the walls. A massive wall of windows rested on the opposite side of the expansive foyer, and the floor was so glossy smooth, I more skated in my socks than walked.

"You play tennis now?" I asked when I noticed the courts out back.

The sound of his footsteps filled the giant space. "Nope. Came with the house."

My eyes continued their sweep of the mini amusement park out back. "Golf?"

A one-noted laugh burst from him. "Can you picture me having the patience to put a tiny ball in eighteen tiny holes over the course of an entire afternoon?"

"I don't remember you having the patience to make it through a football game, even after Coach Ward practically promised you his left arm to play a season your sophomore year."

"I preferred other outlets when it came to physical fitness."

My arms crossed. "Not sure getting into fights every week counts as physical fitness."

Chase's mouth moved as we started for the grand staircase. "I was talking about something else. And it definitely fits the criteria."

My face warmed when I realized what he was getting at. He was right. The way my heart had pounded and my body felt spent after, a session in the sack with Chase Lawson had been the most intense workout I'd ever experienced. Including summer harvest.

After making it to the top of the stairs, I could make out the sound of voices coming from one of the hallways.

Chase glanced at the watch on his wrist. "Nearly ten on the dot. I don't know how she does that." He nodded at Dani, who was stationed outside a room, waiting.

When we were a few steps from the door, she slid in front of the entrance, bestowing an entire monologue to Chase in one pointed look.

"I'm going to introduce Emma to everyone. She can leave after that. God knows I would if I could escape three hours of logistics."

Dani cleared her throat, quietly closing the door. "You want to introduce her to everyone on your team looking like this?"

The way she said it made me feel like I was wearing an outfit made of crumpled newspapers and used condom wrappers.

Chase inspected me, clearly not seeing the same thing Dani was. "She looks like a hard-working, down-to-earth girl."

Dani's head shook firmly. "No, she looks like a mess. You introduce her like this, and everyone's going to suspect something." She stepped closer, lifting a neatly shaped eyebrow at Chase. "She doesn't exactly scream Chase Lawson Arm Candy."

My stomach lurched as though I'd taken a punch to it or eaten some bad seafood.

"I'm going to take a shower," I interjected, reaching my limit of two people arguing about my introduction suitability in front of my face. "Then wander around the amusement park you've got here and check out the sites. I'll catch up with you later."

I started down the hallway, stopping when I realized I had no idea where I was going.

When I glanced back, I kind of wanted to slap the amused look off of Chase's face. "Next intersection, take a right. You can pick whichever room you like best."

"I had the green room prepared for her," Dani said.

"Whatever room you want," he said to me. "Just not mine." When he noticed my puzzled look, he added, "You wouldn't like the mattress. It's too hard for you."

"I don't think it's just the mattress that wouldn't fit my tastes," I threw back before offering a private smile and continuing down the hall.

The green room was the first room in the hall Chase had directed me to. It was perfect for a great-grandmother or a cloistered nun. I could see why Dani had selected that room for me.

After exploring the five guest rooms in the hall, I settled on the one at the very end, mainly because it had the best view of the grounds. It didn't hurt that it had a giant jet tub in the attached bathroom either.

I spent the rest of the day in total relaxation, only enhanced by the tub of cotton candy Chase made sure was delivered to me. I couldn't remember the last time I'd spent a day doing pretty much nothing. Unless you count soaking in a tub teaming with lavender-scented bubbles; having lunch delivered to my room, complete with a linen napkin and a pretty blue flower resting inside a

crystal vase; and spending several hours wandering
the grounds, feeling as though I'd found myself in
some secret garden instead of a private yard in
Nashville.

By nighttime, I'd explored most of the property,
but I'd saved the pool for last. Night swims were my
favorite, and Chase's pool was the kind one would
expect to find on the cover of a home décor magazine. Trudging down the pathway, wearing the
billowy white robe that had been hanging in the
closet, I heard voices coming from the pool's
direction.

I'd hoped to have it to myself, but when I made
out one of the voices, my disappointment eased. I
came around the corner and saw Chase in the spa,
his arms sprawled out along the ledge, chatting with
some woman who, at first, I thought was Dani in
fitness apparel. It wasn't until I heard her voice—
bubbly and bright—that I realized it wasn't.

When Chase caught sight of me, his mouth
stretched into a smile, that one dimple on his right
cheek setting deep. "Miss me?"

The temporary allure of seeing him in a hot
tub, grinning at me, extinguished the moment he
opened his mouth.

"Oh to have the inflated ego you do," I chided,

grabbing one of the navy-and-white striped pool towels from a stack nested beside the chairs. From the looks of it, he was hosting a pool party with half of Nashville invited.

"It's a gift," he replied, before waving at the woman as she walked away.

As she passed me, I saw genuine warmness in her smile. Definitely not Dani. I couldn't help doing a double-take. Petite, blond, green-eyed. They could have been sisters.

"That's Teresa," Chase explained, guessing my thoughts. "She's my personal trainer. She might look tiny and innocent, but she kicks my ass more than any muscled meathead ever has." He rolled his neck a couple of times. "This hot tub is used more for recovery than enjoyment."

"Private trainers. Personal chefs. A hot tub that could fit two dozen adoring fans in skimpy bikinis. Must be hard being you." I unknotted the bathrobe's belt but hesitated taking it off.

"Did you have dinner?" he asked me.

"Carne asada tacos and a chile-lime avocado salad. It was pretty much the best meal I've ever had."

"Mel's an incredible chef. Except when it comes to my meals leading up to a tour or photo shoot."

Settled on the deck beside him was a plate of food that had gone untouched.

Moving closer, I made out three different veggies in varying shades of green and an unappetizing-looking chicken breast. My nose curled when I realized one of the veggies was kale. "Pretty sure they feed the models walking fashion week better than that."

"Pretty sure those models don't eat nothing but junk during the off-season like I do." He stabbed the steamed broccoli with his fork. "My people have it on good authority that a chubby Chase Lawson wouldn't sell out as many stadiums or as many records as a beefcake Chase Lawson."

"It's a cruel world."

He laughed before popping a chunk of chicken into his mouth. "How was your day?"

"Pretty great. How about yours?"

"Non-stop meetings, two grinding workouts, and a conveyor belt of coniferous veggies and lean proteins shoved in my face all day." His head tipped as I moved closer. "Safe to say your day was better than mine."

Sitting on the pool deck across from him, I dipped my feet in the hot, bubbling water. "Yeah, I can't find it in my heart to work up any sympathy for you."

"What do you think? It's nice, right?" His arm swept out at the estate behind us, its hundreds of windows glowing gold.

"You don't need my confirmation that this place is 'nice,'" I said. "But I can't not bring up the little fact that there are children dying of starvation, curable diseases, and civil wars all over the world . . . while you luxuriate in your sprawling palace."

His eyes met mine. "I know. And that's why I donate so much of my money to those charities. I can have last year's spreadsheet of where and how much money I gave emailed to you if it would ease your conscience."

"You could live in a place a tenth the size of this one and have even more to give. Oh, and let's not mention the number of cars you have in that museum you call a garage. How many cars can a person drive at one time? Because last I checked, it was just one." I splashed some water in his direction with my foot.

He splashed back a few drops. "This place, the cars, the plane, all of that is selling an image. Fans wouldn't find me nearly as interesting if I lived in a two-thousand-square-foot home and drove a crossover to the recording studio. Or if I was just another body stuffed in coach class heading to my next concert. All of this, it's selling a fantasy. It comes with the territory."

I found myself looking at the estate with a new set of eyes. "I guess so."

Chase took a few more bites of his dinner before shoving the plate away with a sigh. "I'll give you anything you want if you order a cheeseburger and fries from Mel and give it to me."

I clucked my tongue, rising from the hot tub. "Someone's got to fit in their skinny jeans by next week so all the groupies can go wild over the sight of your ass."

"Ice. Cold," he called as I headed for the pool.

I found myself pausing once more when I went to take off my robe. I was wearing a practical navy one-piece I'd had for a couple years. Not at all exposing or flattering, but the thought of Chase seeing me in a swimsuit had my stomach knotting.

"You're not scared of me seeing you in a swimsuit, are you?" Chase bellowed, reading my damn mind. "Because in case you forgot, I've seen you in a lot less."

My head whipped in his direction, eyes narrowing. "I'm cold."

"It's eighty degrees, you're draped in about five pounds of terry cotton, and you're *cold*?" His brows pulled together. "The pool's heated to a balmy eight-eight, which is at least fifteen degrees warmer than that creek you loved to swim in back home, princess."

My eyes narrowed farther. He used to call me princess whenever I balked at some challenge or exhibited even the slightest of fragile tendencies. I'd hated it back then too.

"You're the one whining about achy muscles from a little workout and a healthy meal that's been prepared for his highness." I slid out of that bathrobe so fast. "We both know who the princess is here."

"Ice. Cold," he repeated, his gaze roaming me now that I'd mustered the courage to shed the robe.

"You can at least attempt to be subtle with your staring." I stepped into the pool, descending the steps until I was halfway in the water. It was pleasantly warm and so clear the water seemed to sparkle.

"Subtlety's never been my strong point. Especially when it came to you." Chase pushed up out of the hot tub and sat on the edge. "You look good, Emma. Real good."

I rolled my eyes at him despite the flutter in my stomach. "That's what all the boys tell me when I slip into my modest-coverage one-piece."

After sucking in a breath, I dove beneath the water and swam toward the opposite end. Surfacing, I wiped the water from my eyes and discovered the hot tub was empty. Chase was standing at the edge of the pool, watching me, the shimmer from the water reflecting against him.

"What are you doing?" I asked.

"Watching you."

Treading water, I gave him a look. "You realize that sounds hardcore creepy, right?"

"You realize who you're talking to, right?"

I sighed, trying not to gawk at his chest. Or his abs. Or his arms. Or insert any other part of his body here. Whatever they'd been feeding him was working. "An eight-year-old boy trapped in a man's body?"

"Speaking of . . ." A spark flashed in his eyes right before he hurled into the air. "CANNONBALL!"

When he hit the water, a deluge of water exploded, spilling over my head. I was still sputtering from the aftermath when he resurfaced.

"I was really looking forward to a peaceful night swim."

"I can do peaceful." He swam closer, water dripping from his hair.

My mind fogged the closer he got, so I put some distance between us. "The only time you've ever been capable of being peaceful was when you were asleep."

"I'm about to prove you wrong," he said right before sealing his lips. Lifting his hand out of the water, he counted off the time on his fingers.

"Ten seconds. Congratulations," I said as he swam closer.

He kept treading closer while I continued my retreat until I could go no farther. My back butted into the pool corner as Chase's arms on either side blocked my getaway. He didn't do anything; he didn't say anything. His eyes met mine, remaining there until my lungs strained.

"Okay, you've proved your point. You can be quiet." When I went to push past him, his arm wouldn't budge. "Move."

"We've got to go over something first," he said, smirking at my efforts to budge his arm.

"What?" I asked, annoyed.

"We're going to be a couple in the public's eyes.

Which means we're going to have to do certain things that couples do."

I blinked at him. "Couples don't do *that* in public. At least not the normal ones."

He gave a grunt of disbelief. "I'm not talking about sex."

"Then what are you talking about?" My voice was rising the more flustered I became. The lack of apparel, the warm water, the way Chase's brown eyes seemed to melt when he looked at me a certain way . . . I was struggling to keep my composure.

"Kissing." He shrugged as though it were obvious. "We've had ten years to get rusty. We don't want to look like a couple of fumbling amateurs when we kiss in public for the first time."

My mouth fell open a little as I tried to determine if he was serious. "Kissing is like riding a bike. We don't need to practice to get it right."

The corners of Chase's eyes creased. "It's more like riding a unicycle. Once you figure it out, with enough consistency, no problem. But if you go a decade without climbing on that unicycle, you're starting right back at square one."

I had to bite the inside of my cheek to keep from laughing. "You're comparing kissing to a unicycle. You're just as romantic as I remember."

Chase treaded closer until my legs were brushing against his with each kick. "Come on. One kiss. Practice makes perfect." His arms drew in, entombing me in his presence. One brow carved into his forehead. "That is, unless you're scared to kiss me in private, half-naked in a swimming pool, because you still harbor some kind of feelings for me . . ."

I shoved his chest as a snap reaction, realizing too late that I should not touch him when he was this close, when I was this conflicted. "Fame has really gone to your head."

His shoulders rose above the water before dipping below again. "So? Prove me wrong."

"Fine." The word materialized on its own. "But if you even try slipping me tongue, my knee is winding up in your groin."

He wet his lips, fighting a smile. "When have I ever complained about any part of you nestling down there?"

My hands balled at my sides as I attempted to approach this whole thing like a science experiment. Objectively. Neutrally. Emotionlessly. "Just kiss me and get it over with."

His smile quirked. "Once you're finished whispering sweet nothings into my ear."

When I tried to push him away, his hands circled my wrists. Chase's eyes found mine, the color of his irises nearly indistinguishable from his pupils. My chest moved quickly when he swam closer, his head angling as his lips aligned with mine.

He hadn't even kissed me and I'd lost all sense of direction. Up was as good as down in my present state. His breath fanned across my lips as he waited, perfectly at ease having me trapped in the corner of his pool, our mouths a sliver of air apart.

His grip on my wrists relaxed right before his mouth finally connected with mine. My body froze the instant he kissed me, but it didn't last long, seeming to melt one piece at a time.

I didn't realize I was sinking until Chase's arm cinched around me, pulling my shoulders back above the water, his mouth not missing a beat. The last piece of me to unthaw was my lips, but the moment they did, they matched his urgency. My arms wound behind his neck as I drew closer, our bodies tangling beneath the water as he kissed me in a way I hadn't been kissed in years; in the kind of way that made a girl feel delicate and invincible at the same time.

Chase treaded water, holding us both above the

surface, the planes of his chest rising to meet mine with our uneven breaths. Before I knew it, our tongues were tying together, though it wasn't him who'd broken that rule first. His chest rumbled against mine as my mouth and hands grew more feverish, no longer under the constraint of my better judgment.

Kissing Chase was exactly as I remembered, yet totally different. The scrape of his calloused fingers against my skin felt the same, yet there was a newfound strength to it. His full lips moved with mine in a dance we'd mastered years ago, but there was a resolve I'd never tasted so deeply before. The way he held me was exactly the same, though the contours of his body had changed.

When my chest was hammering from breathlessness, Chase broke the kiss, managing to evade my ensuing advances. His eyes remained closed for a minute, droplets of water winding down his face from where my hands had been.

When his eyes finally opened, the look in them made my head dizzy, even as I reminded myself this had been a practice kiss. Nothing more.

"How was that?" he asked.

I had to look away in order to make my answer seem convincing. My shoulder lifted out of the water as I shaped my most detached expression. "You were right. Like riding a unicycle."

"No, you were right." Chase's hand drifted up my back, his rough fingertips somehow soft against my skin. "Kissing you is like riding a bicycle."

**4**

---

"You kissed him?" On the other end of the line, Jesse sounded like she'd swallowed an apple whole.

"It was nothing. One tiny practice kiss before we're expected to pucker up in front of a bunch of strangers." I double-checked my suitcase to make sure I'd packed everything I'd need for the next six months on the road. But how did a girl prepare for something like that? Especially when the longest road trip I'd taken had been to Sante Fe for a three-day weekend. "It was the intimacy equivalent of high-fiving him."

"Except you did it with your lips."

My face heated, playing back the scene in my head. "It wasn't like that."

"Sure, it wasn't. What are you going to tell me next? You two worked in a practice screw and it was like sharing a wink?"

I held in the groan, chastising myself for experiencing a weak moment and dishing the truth to Jesse about Chase and me. She'd been sworn to secrecy though, and I'd only told her because she knew how to keep a secret. "How's everyone?" I asked, eager to focus the attention elsewhere.

"Everyone's good. Stunned that you're back together with that derelict, but don't worry, I didn't spill the behind-the-scenes story."

After zipping my suitcase, I made my bed. One of the maids had insisted that she was there to take care of those kinds of things, but my conscience wouldn't allow another human to make the bed I'd slept in when I was more than capable.

"I'm sorry you have to keep it a secret," I said. "I wasn't supposed to say anything, but I had to tell one of you guys. And you were always the best one at keeping a secret."

"Except this secret is major, Em. Chase Lawson is paying you seven figures to be his pretend girlfriend. He is not the kind of guy who needs to pay girls for their company, if you know what I mean."

My grip tightened around the plush white

comforter. The past few days since arriving, I'd witnessed a group of girls lined outside Chase's gate, holding signs with offers ranging from flashing him for a chorus line to bearing his firstborn. Security had tackled one daring woman who'd scaled the gates and made it halfway up the front drive, and yet one more hardcore fan had shown up in her birthday suit and her guitar, singing a unique version of "Goodbye Tales," one of Chase's breakthrough hits.

"You got the tickets I emailed you?" I asked.

Jesse squeed. "*Front row* seats? Yeah, I got them and everyone says a ginormous thank you. Johnny actually suggested selling the tickets and using the money to remodeled the kitchen."

"You should do it. Sold-out front row tickets will sell for a primo price. Besides, you've both heard Chase sing and play a guitar plenty of times."

"Yeah, but never as one of the most popular musical artists at present." She huffed. "The kitchen doesn't need a remodel that bad."

A knock sounded outside my door, and there was no shortage of people who could have been on the other side. Between maids, chefs, assistants, and security guards, this place was a revolving door of bodies.

"Hey, I gotta go," I said.

"Is Chase beckoning or calling?"

"I told you. I'm *not* his beck-and-call girl."

"That's right, you're his pretend girlfriend he makes out with inside of swimming pools under the ploy of practice makes perfect." The sarcasm was thick in her voice.

"It's good to have friends," I muttered, heading for the door when knock number two came. This one not so gentle.

"And it's great to have friends who tell it like it is," Jesse chimed. "Love you and goodbye 'til next time."

"Love you too," I said before hanging up.

On the other side of the door was someone I'd tried avoiding at all costs. I'd see her coming down the same hall and I'd duck into whatever room or closet was nearest. I'd hear the unique crack of her heels and I'd go running the opposite direction.

"Hey, Dani," I greeted, smile and all.

She held out a manila folder, all business. "You're going to need some new clothes for the tour. There's a list of what you'll need, a catalogue of suggested stores, along with a credit card. If you have any questions, you can reach me on my cell."

She was already turning to leave when I cleared

my throat. "I brought clothes. Why do I need to go buy new ones?"

Dani's stare as she inspected my outfit for today needed no interpretation. "You'll need formal attire. Items you can wear out in public. There'll be cameras coming from every direction, fifty deep, when you're at Chase's side. We wouldn't want to shatter any of them with your Country Barbie wardrobe."

My mouth fell open as I floundered to produce a comeback worthy of Country Barbie, but I had to give credit where credit was due. Dani had mastered the talent of insults.

"Would you like to have a driver take you or would you prefer to drive yourself?" she asked, her finger ready to punch a number into her phone.

"I'll drive myself," I said, shaking the folder. "Tell me there's an address for a Country Barbie Fantasy store in here."

"Bergdorf Goodman is as country as it gets." Her eyes did that quick, yet thorough inspection again. "Good luck."

After making a face at her retreating figure, I retrieved my phone and purse so I could get going. Navigating Nashville would be a challenge for a small-town girl from a place where there were no such things as merging lanes or roundabouts, not to mention navigating through a store solely dedicated to clothing instead of the one-stop-shop varieties like back home.

When I made it to the garage—which was nicer than plenty of people's living spaces—I found a long peg of hooks holding a dozen different keys. I wasn't familiar with some of the makes—I wasn't sure if I could even pronounce them correctly—so I went with one I was familiar with.

The big Chevy was the nicest truck I'd ever seen and definitely not intended for farm use. It smelled like Chase—that heady combination of his after-shave and cologne—and it made me wonder if this was the vehicle he used more than the others.

I might have been used to trucks, but once I was driving down the streets of Nashville, I wished I'd gone with the smallest possible option. Between all of the cars and people, weaving up and down streets without hitting anything was more chal-lenging than it should have been.

By the time I made it to the shopping area Dani had highlighted in the folder, my knuckles were white and my nerves frazzled. After squeezing into a parking spot, I flipped through the rest of the information in the folder. There was a glossy black credit card paper-clipped to a check-off list of items for me to pick up. It wasn't a short list.

Eight cocktail dresses, five formal gowns, twenty work-casual outfits, shoes to match every outfit . . . then there were accessories and specific underwear based upon the outfit's design. I was bushed and I hadn't stepped foot inside a store.

Giving myself a pep talk, I leapt out of the truck with the goal of setting some shopping speed records today.

EIGHT HOURS, TWO STOPS AT THE SPECIALTY cupcake shop, and three headaches later, I'd done it. Not sure it was any kind of record based on the professional shoppers who seemed to know exactly what they wanted and didn't need to check the tag for the size or price, but I'd exceeded my own expectations by simply checking everything off of the list. And surviving.

It was dark by the time I maneuvered the truck back into its designated spot in the garage. Thankfully, one of the house supervisors was there to greet me and help wrangle all of my bags up to my room. Once everything was spread out on my bed—all of the bags took up the whole thing and even some of the space on the floor—I realized I had nothing to pack it into for our departure tomorrow.

"Suitcases," I muttered, finding a small scrap of pleasure that Dani wasn't as perfectly organized as one thought.

I guessed there had to be some spare luggage somewhere inside this labyrinth of rooms and closets, so I went on the hunt. When I popped inside a large room at the end of one of the halls, I startled. Not from the surprise of seeing him, but the shock of watching what he was doing and how he looked doing it.

"Hey. Sorry to interrupt," I said when his trainer noticed me hovering in the doorway.

Chase finished his rep then racked the bar loaded with some seriously heavy-looking plates. "Interrupt anytime."

He took the towel Theresa was holding for him and wiped his face before moving on to his shoulders and arms. He wasn't wearing a shirt, and the one article of clothing he did have on looked as if it was about to fall down if it inched any lower down his hips. Shiny, sweaty, and smiling.

My throat burned from the sight of him.

"Did you need something?" He gave me a funny look. Probably because I was gawking at him like he was an ice-cold beverage and I'd crossed the Sahara on foot.

"Suitcase," I said, sounding like an idiot. Licking my lips, I tried again. Diverting my eyes helped so I could speak in more than one-word sentences. "I was looking for a couple of extra suitcases. Do you know where any might be?"

Chase grabbed the water bottle resting on the bench beside him, throwing the towel over one shoulder. "I've got a few spares in my room." He squirted some water into his mouth. "Theresa, you kicked my ass enough for one day?"

"I don't know. You're still standing," she teased before waving him off. "I suppose you can sneak out early. I'll just tailor your next workout so you leave in tears."

"So pretty much every workout except for tonight's?" Chase's pace picked up, and he waved at me to get out so we could make an escape.

Theresa said good night to us both, then she lunged onto a tall bar and whipped out pull-ups like she was GI Jane.

"Good timing," he said after joining me in the hall. "It's like you could hear my muscles weeping in pain."

I stepped aside, giving myself a margin of space

from him. Like this, to me, he was pretty much country-girl catnip.

"So? Did you kale and cardio your way into your skinny jeans?" I asked, hoping I didn't sound as flustered as I felt.

He pointed at his abs as if they said it all. In fairness, they did say a hell of a lot. "Nailed it."

"Nice work." I grimaced at my response. *Nice work?*

"So how was the shopping? Sounded like Dani gave you one hell of a list. I probably should have warned you." He nudged me with his bare, sweaty, muscled arm. "I know how much you hate shopping."

"It was fine. I made it without sustaining too much long-term emotional trauma." He slowed when we turned down the next hall. "I didn't really think about all of the stuff we'd be doing while you're on tour. If I had, I would have realized four pairs of jeans and a black pencil skirt wasn't going to cut it."

His shoulder lifted. "It wouldn't matter. When people look at you, they aren't paying attention to your clothes."

"I think that's a compliment, so thanks?" I said when we stopped outside a door.

"All I mean is that you're beautiful no matter what you wear. Holey jeans or formal gown." He motioned at me as though I was proving his point in my makeshift pajamas consisting of a shirt so worn it was porous, and a pair of shorts that had at one time been sweatpants.

"I'll just wait here," I said when he opened the door and stepped inside his room.

"You can come inside, you know? It's not like you're going to explode into a pillar of fire if you step foot inside the bedroom of a man you aren't married to. Contrary to what that old Methodist church tried convincing everyone of."

"If that was the measure for spontaneous combustion, I would have been ashes years ago." Showing him I wasn't scared, I walked a step inside his room.

"A whole foot inside. You heathen." He clucked his tongue as he loped toward what looked to be a closet.

His room was massive—less of a bedroom and more of a mini house. His bed was tucked into the far end of the room, but chairs and a sofa were settled around the rest. A mini fridge and microwave were built into a granite counter. From the looks of it, Chase could survive in his room for days if he needed to.

I was finishing my inspection when I saw it. His old guitar. His first one. The guitar I'd surprised him with on his fifteenth birthday after stowing away money from babysitting and odd farm jobs for weeks.

"You still have it," I said when I realized he'd returned from the closet and was watching me.

"Of course." His expression relaxed when his eyes fell on the guitar. "It's the best damn guitar I've ever had. Doesn't matter how many new ones I've gotten or how much they've cost, nothing can measure up to my first." When his eyes traced the line between the guitar and me, there was something unrecognizable in them. He held up a couple of large suitcases. "Will these work?"

"Yeah." I nodded. "Except whose initials are those?"

Chase glanced at the tan-and-brown mono-grammed suitcases. "Some French dude's, I think. Don't know for sure. Dani buys most of my stuff for me." He set them down beside me. "I hate shopping almost as much as you do."

"Thanks for the suitcases." I reached for them, but he lifted his hand.

"I've been working on a couple new songs for my next album." He wandered toward his old guitar. "Want to hear what I've got so far?"

My throat knotted before I shook my head. I used to love listening to Chase sing and strum chords on his guitar, but that was a lifetime ago. There was no room for the past in the present.

"You're going to be singing for the next six months. You better save your voice when you can." I reached for the cases again but didn't make it far.

"You want to watch a movie?" Chase asked, padding toward the giant flat screen attached to the wall across from the sofa.

My forehead creased. "A movie?"

"Yeah. One of those things we watch for entertainment's sake, beginning, middle, and end. All different genres." He snapped his fingers as he opened a cabinet containing rows of DVDs. "Speaking of . . . what are you in the mood for?"

"It's almost eleven o'clock," I said.

"We don't have a curfew anymore. We can stay up as late as we want now," he whispered like he was telling me a secret.

"We have to be ready to leave at six in the morning. Or else Dani will probably throw a bucket of cold water on us and drag us out by our ears."

Chase's head tipped back and forth as though he were in agreement. "I never sleep the night before a tour kicks off. I don't even try anymore. I usually wind up watching movies on my own all night, but a partner in crime would be a welcome change." When he noticed me stalling, working it out on my lip, he added, "I've got a stockpile of snacks and drinks. And pretty much any movie you can name."

My better judgment had a different answer than the one I gave him. "Okay."

For a moment, he looked surprised, but not for long. "What do you want to drink?" he asked, backing toward the kitchenette.

"What are you having?"

"What do I want to have or what am I actually going to drink?" he asked.

"Eh, both?"

He swung open the mini-fridge door. "I'm *having* a sparkling water with lime." He shook the glass bottle of Perrier at me. "What I'd nearly, at this point, kill to have is a cherry Coke with extra cherries."

My mouth tugged at the corners. "You still drink cherry Coke?"

He blinked at me, feigning offense. "The way

you said that leads me to the conclusion you think cherry Coke is a taste someone should outgrow."

"Yet here you are, all grown up and drinking a sparkling water instead," I teased as he poured the bottle over a glass of ice. "I'll have the same."

"You don't have to just because I am. I don't need your pity."

I wandered toward the couch, admiring the view of his back. "Fine. I'll take a cherry Coke with extra cherries."

"Sparkling water it is." Even as he said it, he retrieved a can of cola from the fridge, digging the jar of maraschino cherries out right after.

"I haven't seen you have a single drink. Alcohol on the non-approved list of diet foods?" I asked, scanning the fridge for contents other than water and soda. None could be found.

Chase froze in the middle of slicing his lime, the muscles tensing in his shoulders. When he glanced back at me, everything seemed to relax. "I gave that up a year ago," he said. Slowly. "When I drove my truck into a parked minivan after drinking enough whiskey to get six men my size good and drunk. Getting hauled away in the back of a police car and seeing my old man reflecting back when I looked in the mirror scared me straight."

I didn't know what to say. I, like every other non-hermit in the country, had heard the news splashed across the tabloids when Chase got arrested for drunk driving last year. Part of me had been surprised, knowing how much abuse he'd taken from his drunk of a father. Part of me had tried to convince myself I didn't care.

"You never drank back home," I said, tucking my leg beneath me as I sat on the couch.

"That changed when I left."

"The pressures of fame and fortune drove you to drink?" I guessed.

He dropped a handful of cherries into my cola. "No," he said, his head lowering. "But my regrets did."

My eyebrows knitted together. "Regrets like what? Waving goodbye to that run-down doublewide?"

Chase turned around, coming toward me. Handing me my Coke, his fingers lingered when mine wrapped around the glass. "Leaving you."

A tingle wound down my spine. "You don't have to say that in some kind of attempt to apologize. I moved on. I get it. I mean, look at you. You made it."

He came around the front of the couch, staring

at the space beside me as though he were unsure if he could sit there. "No amount of fame was worth the cost of losing you."

"You say that now, but you didn't feel that way eleven years ago."

Instead of sitting, he went to grab the remote. "Part of me knew I'd drag you down with me if I stayed. I knew you deserved more than some dumb-shit with a messed up past and questionable future. I saw an easy way out, and I took it."

Talking about this was ripping open old scars. Wounds I thought had healed years ago. "You were a coward."

Chase's head shook once. "Letting you go was the bravest thing I've ever done."

My gaze wandered toward the door, my mind warning me it was time to leave. My heart was telling me something else entirety.

"I thought we were going to watch a movie," I said, patting the empty half of the sofa.

Chase crashed beside me without stalling. He punched the remote to turn on the television. "What are you in the mood for?"

"After that heavy moment?" I clinked my glass to his. "A comedy."

"Perfect. I still have *Tommy Boy* in the player."

He took a drink of his sparkling water, eyeing my Coke jealously.

I held it toward him, shaking it gently so the ice clinked against the glass. "I won't tell."

Chase didn't pause when he took my glass, taking a long drink. When he finished, he gave a satisfied groan. "This, right here, is a perfect night."

His arm bent behind my back as the movie played.

**5**

I woke slowly, then with a start.

Crap. I'd fallen asleep.

Late at night.

In Chase's bedroom.

My head whipped around, but he was nowhere in sight. The end credits were playing to *Black Sheep*, the second movie he'd popped in and the one I'd fallen asleep during.

"Hey, you're awake." His voice rumbled behind me.

When I spun around on the couch, my eyes bulged. "Hey, you're naked." My eyes clamped shut for a moment before opening. Closed. Open.

"I'm wearing a towel. Not the definition of

naked." Chase gave me a funny look, pointing at the plush white towel cinched at his waist.

"But you're naked beneath it," I argued, wondering why my voice was so high. Must have been the combination of sugary beverage and sleep deprivation.

"Are you okay, Em?"

"I will be when you put some clothes on." My voice managed another octave higher. "And why did you take a shower while I was asleep?"

"Do you want me to answer that how I *should*? Or why I actually took one?" he asked, rubbing the back of his neck.

"You already know my answer." I blinked, trying to clear the sleep from my eyes.

Chase's mouth clamped shut right after it opened.

"Just spit it out," I said.

"I'm trying to think of a better way to put it, but I'm coming up empty in the options department."

"Since when did you feel like you needed to censor yourself around me?" I asked, wincing when I felt my leg tingling from having fallen asleep.

His expression read *what the hell* as he took a breath. "A shower was a better alternative than nursing a hard-on all night with you curled up beside me."

My eyes inadvertently dipped south of his towel line, while my mind grappled to restart. "Chase . . ."

"Sorry if that offends your delicate sensibilities, *princess*"—he smirked when I narrowed my eyes at him—"but that's the truth. It's what I feel when I'm around you. I want you, Em." His arms shot in my direction. "My mind knows I don't stand a chance, but my body doesn't give a fuck about the odds."

My chest depressed as though someone was stepping on it. "You left me in pieces when you disappeared."

"I know." His hand ran through his wet hair as he stared at the floor, his forehead drawn. "You'll leave me in pieces this time when you leave."

"How do you know I'll leave?"

"How do you know the sun will rise?" His chest moved with his breath. "Some things are absolute."

My fingers rubbed my forehead as I struggled to make sense of what was happening, as I resisted accepting the feelings surging to the surface inside. "We had our chance. It didn't work."

"I'm a big believer in second chances. Kind of an important policy to adopt when you're as big of a screw-up as I am." His hands wrapped around the back of his neck. "I want a second chance with the first woman I ever loved."

My eyes closed at his confession. Chase always had a way with words—it was why he was such a successful singer/songwriter. He could knit words together in a way that could make a person feel any or every emotion a human being was capable of. Lord knew I was experiencing half a dozen right now.

*Get up and walk away. Nothing is worth feeling that kind of broken again.* The warnings kept coming, even as I tasted the words in the back of my mouth. "I can't give you everything," I whispered, shifting on the couch.

He stepped closer. "I'll take whatever you can."

"Six months. No promises. No professions," I listed, as though my subconscious had been devising this proposal for months.

"Deal." Chase didn't give the air a chance to still before answering.

"That was too fast," I said, realizing I should have made the terms more stringent.

His head tipped at me. "Have you ever met a beggar who refused what was offered?"

"You're Chase Lawson. Not a beggar."

He moved closer, this time not stopping. "I am where you're concerned." He didn't stop until he was in front of the couch, hovering above me, a glint in his eyes I hadn't seen in years—the kind that made every part of my body twitch in anticipation.

"What are you doing?" My words came out sounding breathless.

"I've got six months. I'm not wasting a single day. Not one hour." His arms circled me, drawing me to him before lifting me from the couch.

My heart elevated into my throat from feeling him against me, feeling myself against him. "Chase —" My voice broke as he moved in long strides toward his bed. My gaze landed on the clock resting on his dresser. "It's too late."

His face aligned in front of mine. "No," he said, his lips just touching mine. "It's not."

My skin prickled from the earnestness in his words. "I didn't realize agreeing to this messed-up proposal would mean falling into bed with you five seconds later."

"You're not in my bed." His mouth curled up playfully. "*Yet.*" His arms released, sending me spilling onto the mattress below him.

"Chase," I exhaled . . . a warning . . . a welcome.

"You know I love hearing my name on your lips when we're in bed." His fingers traced the shape of my lips, then dragged down the half-open seam.

"What are we doing?" I asked as his other hand slid up my thigh, slipping inside my shorts, skimming even higher.

"Making up for the last ten years." He leaned over me, his eyes lingering above mine.

A sharp sound escaped from my mouth when he touched me, his finger drawing lazy circles before slowly pushing inside.

My back arched as my hands curled into fists around his comforter. Wanting Chase in any way should have felt wrong—criminal even—but everything felt right. From the way he was looking at me, to the way he was touching me. It felt right in the kind of way that makes a person question if they'd ever truly been right about anything else before this.

When his finger could go no farther, he held there, his eyes excited. Then a wide smile stretched into place.

"Pleased with yourself?" I asked.

He nodded slowly, his hair raining a few drops of water onto my cheeks. "Good to know your body still reacts to mine the same way mine does to yours." His finger curled inside me as he pulled out, making my head roll back into the pillow.

"Maybe I was having a really naughty dream that got me all hot and bothered," I teased.

"Or maybe I emerged from the shower all hard and wet and that got you hot and bothered." His grin took on a wolfish slant as he wiped his finger on the inside of my thigh, proving his point.

"Are you going to keep congratulating yourself for turning me on?" My eyes challenged him as I leaned up on my elbows. "Or are you going to do something about it?"

His mouth lowered to my ear. "You were my girl long enough to know the answer to that."

Before he finished, his fingers pushed back inside me, finding a rhythm that had my breath coming in uneven pants as my fists grappled for a stronghold in his comforter.

"I want your hands on me," he ordered, his breath hot against my neck. "Hit, scratch, stroke, slap, just put them on me."

My hands transferred to him, securing into the grooves of his shoulders. As his fingers penetrated me, drawing me dangerously close to the edge, his thumb circled my clit.

"Don't close your eyes."

I forced them back open, finding his face hanging directly above mine. There was a look on his face, a shadow in his eyes that was almost frightening. It was how Chase made love—with the power of a predator.

"Look at me when you come," he husked, the sinews of his neck pressing through his skin as though he were on the cusp of his own climax.

It hit me hard, without warning. It hit me as though it were breaking me from the shell of the life I'd been living since he'd left. My body froze as the orgasm tore through me, Chase staring at me with rapt fascination, unblinking.

When it was over, a weak stream of air escaped my lips before I collapsed into his arms, my muscles turning to liquid and my inhibitions to vapor.

"Six months," I whispered unevenly.

His mouth lowered, floating just above my lips. "I'd take six seconds."

## 6

A CONVOY OF BLACK, GLEAMING TOUR BUSES waited in the front drive by six the next morning. A convoy. It looked like the whole of country music was going on tour at the same time.

"Isn't this a lot of buses for one singer?" I rambled to one of the house managers helping load the buses.

He motioned at the row of luggage lining the walkway. "Not if you're Chase Lawson." He rushed off to direct the bus drivers.

"It's not like he's the next messiah," I muttered.

"Heard that." A figure leapt out of the bus front and center. Chase came straight for me, lifting his sunglasses onto his head when he was a few feet away. "And from what you were moaning last night, I must be some kind of god."

My mouth opened as I scanned to see if anyone was nearby to have possibly overheard. All clear. "It takes more than fancy finger work to claim divinity. Nice try."

"Obviously. I've got all kinds of plans to earn that title." He leaned in, the ends of his hair grazing my cheek. "All. Kinds."

"We agreed to be discreet," I said.

"As far as everyone knows, save for a select few, we're a couple. We don't need to be discreet about anything."

I stepped back, crossing my arms. "True, but maybe we should tone it down when it comes to hinting at past or future sexual feats, encounters, or challenges in a public setting."

He closed the space between us. "Maybe we should tone nothing down. Especially in the stated category."

"This is all coming too fast." Another step back. "Slow down."

"This has all been a long time coming." His mouth quirked on one side before he took a deliberate step toward me. "Speed up."

A chorus of hoots sounded from down the line of buses. Chase grumbled.

"Who's that?" I asked, inspecting the four guys approaching. They were making the kind of noise a person made when their football team made state.

"The boys in the band."

Chase shoved them away when they clustered around him, throwing insults and jabs. I blinked at the five grown men behaving like unruly adolescents.

The one wearing a Hawaiian shirt unbuttoned with nothing underneath noticed me first. He wrestled away from the cluster, waggling his brows. "Hello, hello. You must be the ex."

Chase huffed. "We're together, moron. How does that make her my ex?"

"She's your ex from the past." Hawaiian shirt guy snapped his fingers. "If you break up again, that will make her your ex-ex-girlfriend." His face creased for a moment. "Do the exes cancel each other out then? So even if you do break up again, she's still your girlfriend? Math isn't my strong suit."

Chase emerged from the cluster, grabbing the collar of the guy's shirt and dragging him away from me a few feet. "Drums aren't either."

The guy covered his chest with his hand, giving Chase a pitiful look. "You wound me."

"If I introduce you assholes to her, do you promise to get back to doing whatever it was before you decided to pester us?" Chase sidled up beside me.

"We can try," one of them answered.

"Good enough," Chase muttered. "Emma, this is Ben, Lane, Sawyer, and Colt," he said it all in one breath, pointing down the line as he went. "Assholes, this is Emma."

They all smiled. A couple winked. "Hey, Emma," they said in unison.

"They might come on kind of strong, and have personal taste issues"—Chase eyed Lane, the Hawaiian-shirt-wearer—"but they're decent guys."

"The kind of guys you'd let date your sister if you had one?" I asked.

Chase's face flattened. "Hell, no."

The guys shared a laugh with me, then Ben slid off his cowboy hat, gracing me with a serious look. "Let me get this straight, Emma. You were together with Chase back in high school?" He paused long enough for me to nod. "So you already had enough experience to know better than to get together with a guy like this?"

Chase's head fell back, more grumbling spilling from him.

My shoulders lifted. "Well, we got to earn our way into heaven somehow."

"I love her." Colt clapped, cracking up. "There's still some chick out there who isn't under the impression Chase Lawson hung the moon. There's hope for humanity."

"I was just thinking I needed to take out a want ad for a new guitarist," Chase chided, steering me toward the bus.

"Good luck with that." Colt held out his arms. "I'm irreplaceable."

"You boys have a nice drive. I'll be enjoying mine minus all the nonstop noise you four make."

"You'll be making your own kind of noise." Lane dodged out of Chase's reach, flashing a toothy grin. "Just keep in mind, you've got a sold-out crowd to sing to tonight. Don't go losing that suggestive baritone from whatever you two love-birds decide to do to pass the next six hundred miles."

"Jealousy's a vice!" Chase hollered after them.

"So is premarital sex. Sinner!"

I couldn't tell if it was Ben or Colt's voice that got the last word in, but their laughs all melded together as they waved goodbye before disappearing into their bus a couple back.

"That wasn't your everyday introduction," I said, stopping outside the bus entrance.

"Yeah, sorry. Adulthood might have evaded every one of them, but they'd give you the shirt off their back if you needed it." The hollows beneath his eyes were shaded from going without sleep last night, but his eyes were bright and clear. A day's worth of stubble framed the lower half of his face, and his lips were just swollen enough to hint at what we'd been doing last night.

My lungs burned from standing this close to him. I flinched when Chase's fingers slid through mine. "They seem great."

"Chase!" Standing beside the luggage, Dani indicated the three bags that were mine. "Which bus do you want hers loaded onto?"

From the way Dani was referring to me, it was like I wasn't even there, not that that was anything new. Her hair was pulled into a crisp bun, and her black skirt suit looked so well starched a wrinkle wouldn't dare settle in.

"Mine," Chase answered before turning to climb the bus stairs, his hand leading me along.

"Yours?" Her tone reeked of disbelief. "You've always ridden alone."

"Up until now."

Dani's heels clacked in our direction. "I don't think it's a good idea."

Chase paused, looking back at Dani. "Why not?"

Her eyes locked on our joined hands. "You don't want to blur the lines between business and pleasure." She spoke slowly, not blinking. "You two have an arrangement. Don't forget that."

Chase was quiet for a moment, probably thinking over what she was hinting at. We'd already blurred the lines. Big time. But only once. We could get back to the original agreement and forget last night had ever happened.

It was impossible though. No matter the past, despite the scars, Chase and I could never be near one another and stave off the desire we felt for the other. It would be the equivalent of telling your lungs to ignore air.

"She's riding with me," he said in a tone that boded no argument.

I followed him into the bus while Dani fired off instructions that my bags were to be loaded onto Chase's bus.

"She likes you, doesn't she?" I asked Chase once we were inside the bus.

He slid out of his worn leather jacket and hung it over the back of a chair. "Dani?"

I answered him with one concentrated look.

"Jealous?"

"Was I ever when all of the girls back home were throwing themselves at you?"

Chase's eyes settled on my hip where I'd planted my hand, following the curve of my body until he reached my eyes. "You never were the jealous type."

"So? Does she like you?"

His head shook. "No. She cares about me, but not like that. It's purely platonic where Dani's feelings are concerned for me."

"How do you know? The way she acts like I'm your personal kryptonite leads me to the conclusion she's into you."

"She's trying to protect me, that's all."

"Protect you?" I motioned at him in all his towering, built goodness. "From me?"

He snapped his fingers at my summation. "Exactly."

"Why do you need to be protected from me?"

"The same reason you're protecting yourself from me." Chase stalked closer, his arms gathering me before I could dodge him. "I'll talk with her. I'll ask her to ease up on you. I'll promise her you're not going to rip my heart out and stomp on it like we both know you're going to do."

"I don't want to hurt you."

"I know." He pulled me to him, inhaling the scent of my hair. "But you will."

The familiar sound of heel strikes entered the bus. When I tried to unfold from his hold, Chase's grip only tightened.

"I'm sorry to interrupt." Dani cleared her throat as she sashayed by us, dropping her briefcase onto the table nestled against the side of the bus. "But I'm going to have to join you two since I had plans to ride with Emma this leg to go over the tour schedule." She was firing up her laptop at the same time she was shuffling through a pile of papers with dates and times listed on them. Her eyes cut to Chase. "Besides, you'll probably want to take the next nine hours to rest anyway. You've got a big night."

"Give me a few minutes to give Em the tour." Chase shot a thumbs-up to the driver who'd just climbed aboard and promptly sealed the door shut.

"It's a tour bus. Not Disneyland," Dani replied,

but she didn't put up any further argument as Chase led me deeper into the bus.

"Fridge, food, et cetera," he said, knocking the stainless steel fridge as we moved through the kitchen area. "Help yourself to whatever. We bring a chef along for meals as needed, but don't exactly ignore the endless drive-thrus we pass either. Basically, if you want something, help yourself. If you find yourself craving a Frosty, let Chip know and he can swing by the closest Wendy's." Chase pointed up front where Chip was settling into his seat.

"Your tour bus looks like the inside of a Four Seasons," I said, studying the seating area that was so neatly arranged, I'd be afraid to relax there for fear of messing up the throw pillows or making footprints in the area rug. "Not that I know from experience what the inside of a Four Seasons looks like."

Chase's shoulder bumped mine. "This is nicer. From someone who's stayed in plenty of Four Seasons.

"Television's behind this wall. The remote there lets you access it and pretty much whatever channel you could want to watch." Chase tapped the wall above the fireplace, but where a television could have been hiding there, I didn't have a clue. "Bathroom is here. Plenty of room to take a shower, bath, or whatever." He slid the door open, waving me inside.

"I can actually turn around in here without hitting my head on something." I extended my arms, doing another spin without touching a thing. "This is slightly more spacious than my grandparents' old motorhome."

Chase made a face. "I had to fold in half to squeeze inside that bathroom."

"Yeah, but it was fun."

Chase slid a sheet of my hair behind my back. "It was." His eyes lost focus for a moment. Then he moved on. "And this back here is the bedroom." He waited for me outside of it, his mouth working when he noticed my hesitation. "Scared?"

My eyes narrowed. "Funny."

Clearing my throat, I slid inside his room, not sure what I'd find. Half of me was expecting to find posters of half-naked women and florescent beer signs. The other half was still out on its verdict.

Instead, I found Chase's room was similar to his room back at his house. Simple, straightforward . . . impersonal. A bed to sleep in, a closet to hang clothes in, a chair to relax in, and that was about it. No pictures, no personal touches that would make me identify this room with what I knew of Chase, no books or magazines to pass long miles and sleepless nights.

"It's nice," I offered when he settled beside me, an expectant look on his face.

"It'll be nicer when you're beside me in that bed." His fingers brushed down my arm. "You still hog the middle? Because I'm good with either side. I'm an ambi-side sleeper."

"There's no such thing as an ambi-side sleeper." My heart picked up when I focused on his bed. Our arrangement struck in private seemed so simple last night, but now, it felt anything but.

"Fine. I can sleep on the left or right. Or top. Or bottom." His dark eyes gleamed. "I don't care just as long as I get to be next to you."

"We'll work that out later." I cleared my throat and slid behind him, out of his room.

"Looking forward to it." He popped open one of the closets in the hall and retrieved his old guitar. "Since it sounds like you're going to be spending the next few hours going over a schedule, I'm going to hang out in here and work on some new songs."

My nose curled as I considered my near future with Dani the Emma Hater. "You're kicking off a tour for your new release. What's the hurry to put out new music?"

Chase lifted the guitar strap behind his head, and the sight of him holding a guitar tested the sturdiness of my knees. "Inspiration doesn't follow release schedules."

"Good luck."

"You too," he called back.

I found Dani stationed at the table, her weapons of scheduling and organization strewn about the table as though she were about to take on the Roman Empire singlehandedly.

"Okay, I'm here. Hit me with the hellfire that will be the next six months." I detoured to the fridge to snag a drink. I probably needed something stronger than a sparkling water for this layover in hell. I set an extra bottle of sparkling water beside Dani. "Something to cool you down."

"I'm freezing already. Chase keeps his tour bus so cold it's like he's trying to keep dead bodies from unthawing." She extended two fingers and slowly pushed the sparkling water away.

When I caught myself about to offer to get her a coffee or a hot cocoa or a warm cup of gratitude, I bit my tongue. I twisted off the cap of my water and chugged half of it before sitting. She might have been freezing, but I was close to my boiling point.

"Let's get this over with," I said as I slid into the booth seat across from her.

Instead of the thick stack of paper I thought she'd be dropping in front of me, she slid a sleek, stylish phone my way. "Your current phone looked like it would malfunction if I tried uploading all of this onto it." She patted the tower of papers before tapping a manicured nail on the large phone screen. "Every contact you could possibly need, every date and time of every event we currently have scheduled which you will be involved in, is loaded on here." She tapped the calendar button and scrolled to a random day, selecting an event that was listed as St. Charles Children's Hospital Gala. "You'll find the dress code in the comments section, along with the numbers of local hair and makeup contacts should you so choose. Arrival times, transportation plans, and expected departure times are all included. I've even included what Chase will be wearing to each event so you'll have the option to complement your wardrobe choice to his."

All I could do was blink at the screen as she scrolled through event after event. "You think of everything, don't you?"

"It's my job to think of everything." She tapped at her tablet then turned it toward me.

It was one of those Hollywood celebrity gossip sites. I knew that from Jesse, whose guilty pleasure was checking out the latest juicy buzz. The headline read "Chase Lawson Gets Back to His Roots," but I didn't read the actual article because I was too fixated on the photo of the two of us attached to it.

We were disembarking his jet the first day I'd arrived in Nashville. Chase was waiting at the bottom of the stairs, staring at me a few steps above him. There was nothing intimate about the photo at all—we weren't even touching—but the intimacy was in the way he was looking at me. In the way I was returning that look.

My stomach caved in on itself, accepting there was no going back now. The news was out.

"That's just one of the many articles that began cropping up yesterday." Dani twisted her tablet around, looking like she was about to scroll to the next one, but I waved her off. It was enough to know the news was out there—I didn't want to see every photo or headline attached to us. "You step out in public, you'll be recognized. You have a phone conversation in an elevator, it's going to be overheard. You have to account for every move-

ment, every word. You'll be scrutinized mercilessly."
She clasped her hands, speaking to me as though
she were addressing Congress. "You won't be able
to wash your hands for fewer than thirty seconds
without the whole world talking about how unhy-
gienic you are. You strike up a random, totally
harmless conversation with a stranger at a coffee
shop, and it will be twisted until you're made to look
like a two-timing floozy."

My hands plastered across the table, I wondered
if the bus was jetting along at mach 3 from the way
my stomach was reacting. "It will be okay," I said, as
much to assure Dani as myself. "I've stayed out of
trouble my whole life and I'm a few years past the
rebellion stage. They want to spin an innocent
exchange, let them. I don't care what they say about
me or how much high esteem the public holds
me in."

"I don't give a damn either, frankly." She leaned
back in her seat, pinning me to mine with her stare.
"But I do care about Chase's, and anything you do
or are perceived to do will reflect directly on him."

"You're saying I have the ability to tarnish
Chase's reputation?" I summed up with a mutter.
"Well there's a role reversal."

She ignored my little quip, glancing over her

shoulder. "One more thing." She blinked at me innocently. "You hurt him, and I will ruin you."

In one seamless movement, Dani rose and walked away.

"Seems fair," I muttered.

The next nine hours passed uneventfully. I chatted with my parents and caught up on the latest happenings. I skimmed through some back issues of *Rolling Stone* magazine I found stuffed in one of the cabinets. Chase and I played a few hours of cards, we ate (I might have slipped him a couple handfuls of Flamin' Cheetos when the gustapo, a.k.a. Dani, wasn't looking), and then we took a nap inadvertently when we fell asleep watching *Brady Bunch* reruns.

Chase must have woken up before me, because when I finally came to, he wasn't stretched out on the couch beside me where he'd been. A blanket had been draped over me, and the lights were dim. Sitting up, I found the bus was parked outside some massive structure. We must have been at the stadium in Dallas.

"Chase?" My voice cracked thanks to my extended nap.

A baritone clearing of a throat came from behind me. "Mr. Lawson is backstage, meeting with

VIPs right now. He asked me to let you know when you woke up."

Twisting around, I found a giant of a man looming toward the front of the bus, dressed in all black, his skin the same ebony tone.

"Please tell me you're on our side." I smiled nervously.

That same deep tenor rumbled in his chuckle. "I'm one of Mr. Lawson's bodyguards."

"Thank goodness, because I would surrender right now if you weren't with us."

"I'm afraid I don't follow, ma'am."

I set aside the blanket and stretched my arms above my head. "Yeah, sorry. It takes a few minutes for the delirious to wear off when I wake up. I should be talking like my typical awkward self soon."

"If you'd like to freshen up before we go in, I've been instructed to escort you backstage whenever you're ready."

Seriously, his voice was so deep, all I could compare it to was the sound a didgeridoo made.

"Ten-four," I said, heading back toward Chase's room. I assumed that was where my luggage had been placed. Since Dani was the queen when it came to thinking of everything.

Another jewel in her crown—my bags had been unpacked and everything hung, folded, or stacked in closets and drawers.

After rushing to change and make some sense of my hair and makeup, I paused in front of the mirror to check my reflection. I'd gone with a short, flowy summer skirt, paired with a white eyelet top, completed by a pair of wedges that made me a whole three inches taller. My hair had a couple of dents I wasn't able to brush out, and my makeup was, at best, a freshman attempt.

I lived in jeans and boots, ponytails and Chap-Stick. It was a rare occasion that called for getting dressed up like this, and when I found myself scrutinizing the shape of my eyebrows, I turned away from the mirror and left. The public could take me as I was and deal with it. I wasn't going to spend eight hours a day waxing, shaping, and sculpting my body to fit a mold that served no purpose other than to look pleasing in a photograph.

"I don't think you mentioned your name," I said as I approached the wall of man stationed in the hallway.

"Everyone in Mr. Lawson's crew calls me Tall Drink."

I motioned at him. "Obviously."

"But my mama calls me Pete, so you can call me either/or."

"Which do you prefer?" I asked.

He motioned for me to wait in the bus as he stepped outside, scanning the area as though he were protecting a foreign diplomat. When it was clear, he waved me out. "It's all the same to me. I'm just glad no one calls me Chicken Legs, String Bean, or Skeletor anymore."

My forehead creased as I examined the size of his biceps again. Close to the size of a tree stump. "People used to call you Skeletor?"

"*People* didn't. Little demon children did back when I was in school." He stayed beside me, his eyes constantly scanning the perimeter.

"Sore subject?" I guessed.

"It's a lot less sore after I showed up to my ten-year reunion and Pencil Petey looked like a dark chocolate Hulk." A chuckle rumbled in his chest as we paused outside a locked door. Pete knocked twice, but it looked more like he was attempting to beat the door in.

When the door swung open, another giant appeared, this one dressed in head-to-toe black as well, but his skin was more of a bronze color.

My hands flew into the air. "I surrender."

The two bodyguards exchanged a look.

Pete lifted his shoulder. "She's strange."

"Awkward was the adjective I used," I corrected before weaving inside the door and following Pete down a long, dark hall. "How many more of you two are there?"

Pete's heavy footsteps rumbled through the concrete tunnel. "Two more on staff. The stadiums provide their own security."

"How much security does one person need?"

"One person named Chase Lawson when he's playing to a sold-out crowd of mostly women under the age of thirty and desperate to carry his child?" The guard behind me clucked his tongue.

"There's a colorful image," I chimed as we emerged from the tunnel into the stadium. My feet froze from the sheer magnitude of it all. Thousands upon thousands of empty seats dotted the perimeter, the dome of the stadium seeming to rise into the stratosphere, it looked so far out of reach. "Every seat in this place is going to be filled soon?"

Pete made a grunt of agreement. "Along with every seat at every stadium we hit on this tour."

My mind couldn't wrap around the reality that the boy who used to serenade me down by the river on summer nights after we made love was the same one that millions of people had purchased tickets to come experience him singing for them.

"Ma'am?" Pete held out his arms in indication of where he wanted me to go, so I unglued my shoes from the floor and followed him.

We climbed the metal stairs up to the stage area, and I could just make out the sound of voices coming from behind the endless wall of curtains. I could make out Chase's in the mix, tangled with mostly female voices.

Hello, VIPs.

The stab I felt in my throat when I walked around the corner and saw them was unusual for me. Jealousy was not an emotion I was prone to, but given there were dozens of young, gorgeous woman waiting in line to meet Chase, I cut myself some slack.

I wasn't sure if I should stand there and wait until he was done or head over, but Chase made my decision easy. He must have noticed me from the corner of his eye—or it could have been the behe-moths on either side of me—because he was already smiling when his head turned toward me. He waved me over, finishing signing an autograph and posing for a picture with a fan who could have been a runway model.

Chase's gaze wandered over me, devouring as he went. I rubbed my forearm to chase away the tingles. When he reached me, he didn't hesitate to gather me to him in what I thought would be a quick embrace. There was nothing quick about it.

"You look amazing," he whispered, his clean-shaven cheek brushing against my temple.

"You look amazing-er," I replied, blinking at the mass of fans waiting for him and staring at his legendary backside. Not that I could blame them. "You know, I'm worried about how tight your jeans and shirt are. You wouldn't want anything cutting off the blood to certain parts of your body."

His hand spread across my lower back, drawing me closer to him. "Any parts in particular you're worried about?"

My throat moved as I tried to ignore the press of his hips against mine, the fit of our bodies together. "All of them?"

His soft laugh rumbled against my chest. "I'll let you strip me down later to check for any signs of impaired circulation. Just make sure you're thorough."

Behind us, I noticed phones lifting, flashes from cameras blinking at us. "Is this for the cameras?" I whispered to him. "Helping improve your public image?"

My head moved in front of his, needing to know what was real and what was for show. For some reason, I needed to be able to distinguish between the two. It would all come to an end in six months, but to endure the next half a year, I needed to know which words and looks were for me, and which were for the scrutinizing public.

"When we're together, it's only us," he said, looking me straight in the eyes.

My attention wandered to the photo-happy fans waiting for their idol. "You picked me to help clean up your image. I just want to know what's real and what's for show."

Chase clasped my face, adjusting my view so it was focused on him. "I chose you for *you*. And every bit of this, you and me, in public or private, on camera or off, is real."

An emotion overcame me then, one I needed to quarantine until it had died off, because I couldn't go down that path again with Chase. Once was enough. I could give him six months of no commitments, boundaries, or promises . . . but I could never again give him my forever.

"You've got some fans to bewilder." I cleared

my throat, winding out of his arms. "And I've got a seat to snag for what I keep hearing should be a decent-enough concert."

Chase huffed. "I'll show you decent."

"I'll be waiting." I held out my arms, backing away.

"But you're not going to be watching from the crowd. You'll be watching from the best seat backstage." Chase pointed down a hall of curtains that led to the stage.

My head shook. "This is my first Chase Lawson concert. I'm not watching it from anywhere other than out there with the rest of the crazed crowd."

Chase folded his arms. "Not safe. You'll watch the concert from backstage or not at all."

I folded my own arms. "I didn't let you boss me around when I was sixteen, and I sure as hell am not going to let you more than a decade later."

The muscles of his neck pressed through the skin. "I'm not bossing you around. I'm merely telling you what's safe and what is not. Your picture is out there now. Fans will recognize you. Things will go down. Stuff will get messy. I'll probably wind up serving ten to twenty for involuntary manslaughter."

My eyes lifted. "No one's going to be looking at

me when you're up there on stage moving your hips the way you do. I'll be fine."

"You're wearing a skirt that will expose your entire ass if you lean over a few inches."

I pointed toward the line of VIPs. "Which is still half a foot longer than most of your diehard fans."

"You're sitting backstage." He clapped his hands, backing away, as though that were the end of it.

My fingers drummed across my arm. "Wanna bet?"

## 7

From the moment he took the stage, I understood. Everything.

The sold-out concerts. The record album sales. The countless magazine covers. The rabid fans. All of it.

Chase, on stage, guitar in hand, singing into a microphone and looking into the crowd like he was baring his soul for any and all to see . . . it took my breath away. He'd always had a good voice, the kind that made you want to close your eyes and gently sway to the beat, but age had refined his voice. Evening out the jagged notes, trussing together the broken harmonies.

Five songs in, and my mouth was hanging half-open, my body still with awe. Everyone else around me was chanting his name, dancing, or singing along, but it took all of my strength to stand there and watch.

I'd gotten my way. Not that I'd doubted I would. Chase might have talked a big game and asserted his alpha tendencies without apology, but I'd always been the exception to that. He could command an army, but he'd never been able to get me to do anything unless I wanted to.

Experiencing this with the rest of the crowd was the only way to see my first Chase Lawson concert. I had a front row seat, and Chase had made sure his personal and the area security were close by if I befell some tragedy like getting beer splashed on my toes or whatever he was so concerned was going to happen.

I caught his gaze wandering to my seat often, though it must have been hard to see me with the bright lights shining up on stage. Every time his eyes found me, his mouth turned up a little higher.

A few songs later, a big dude a few seats down became that "one guy" at every concert. Loud, obnoxious, and over-served. He must have been with his wife or girlfriend, but you never would have guessed it from the way he was talking to her. It got to a point where he was distracting people from the concert, and I wasn't the only one who was uncomfortable with the string of insults and profanities he was firing at the near-cowering woman beside him.

I couldn't stay quiet and pretend to ignore it for another second.

"Hey!" I hollered past the few people between him and me. "Leave her alone already!"

The dude froze in the middle of his latest tirade, blinking at me. "Mind your own business, bitch." He finished what was left in his can of beer before crushing it and dropping it onto the floor.

Resisting the urge to flip him off, I glanced at the woman beside him, who was close to, if not already, shedding tears. "Are you okay?"

"She's fine!" he shouted at me. "But you're not going to be if you don't shut that fucking mouth of yours!"

The people between us were shifting, even more uncomfortable, but no one looked ready to step in and do anything.

"Do you want to come and stand by me?" I asked the woman, who was too afraid to look at me, so I slid past people toward her.

In front of the guardrail, I noticed security easing in, watching the transaction, bodies primed for action. Chase was at the other end of the stage, breaking into the catchy chorus of "Goodbye, Girl."

"Back off." The man lunged in front of the woman before I could reach her, making it a point to stand at his full height. Which wasn't all that intimidating, even at my less-than-impressive stature. He was nothing more than a coward and a poser. The only thing country about him was the make of his boots.

My hands settled on my hips. "No."

"Bitch, you better back away before I make you."

Holding out my arms, I lifted a brow in challenge. "Let's see you try. Coward."

I think it was the coward part that got to him more than anything else. He came at me—I hadn't been expecting that—but before he could take a second step, someone cut in.

It wasn't one of the people in the seats beside us though. It wasn't even one of the security guards. It was the guy on stage who'd leaned over the guardrail and grabbed the guy coming at me. Chase had a good hold on him, dragging him up on stage, the whole time hollering words and phrases that made me thankful he didn't have his mouthpiece on for all to hear. A couple of his personal security rushed onto the stage, taking the guy off Chase's hands before wrestling him off the stage.

The crowd stilled, silence stretching through the stadium. Chase stood there, shoulders still quivering, staring at the spot the guy had been drug off as though he were waiting for him to break free. His posture relaxed after a moment, before he spun around, his eyes landing right on me.

For the briefest second, there was relief. That was replaced by something less relaxed. I felt like a child being scolded by my mom for sneaking too many cookies.

"Ma'am." A giant hand rested on my shoulder from behind. "We can see the rest backstage."

I was about to utter my agreement, but Pete must have thought I was more likely to put up an argument.

"Please don't make me throw you over my shoulder to get you out of here. I like you, but I like my job a whole lot more."

"I'll leave the floor on my own two feet, thank you very much." I shoved by him, heading toward the end of the row and trying to ignore the sharp stare coming at me from up on stage.

Once Chase saw I was in the capable care of the Greek God of Intimidation, he crouched to pick up his guitar. He took one look at it, then held it up as he strolled to the microphone.

"Never bring your guitar to a fight!" he crowed, waving his broken guitar to the roaring crowd. "I think I just thought up a title for my next album."

Someone rushed on stage, carrying a fresh guitar. After adjusting a few strings and wiping his face off with the black handkerchief he had sticking out of his back pocket, he burst into his next song.

"Are you all right, ma'am?" Pete asked once we were tucked backstage.

"Yeah. I'm good," I replied, sneaking a peek out into the crowd. The woman with the empty seat beside her was standing, singing with the crowd and waving her arms. Her face was relaxed, maybe even peaceful. "Actually, I'm great."

"Next time you aim to pick a fight, give me a heads-up first." Pete cracked his neck. "Doesn't look good when the man I'm hired to protect interrupts a sold-out concert to protect the woman he's also paying me to protect."

"I wasn't trying to pick a fight. I was doing what was right," I replied.

"Yeah, well, doing what's right usually comes along with a fight." Even as he gave me a stern look, he was fighting a smile.

I nudged him. "I'll give you a heads-up next time."

We listened to the rest of the concert from backstage, the view of the crowd from this vantage unreal. When Chase came offstage after his last song, his jaw ground when he saw me. He might have just been singing about summer nights and skinny dipping, but he clearly was still pissed at me.

Dani was waiting with a hand towel and a bottle of water, rattling off a few things to him I couldn't hear. He didn't hear any of it; he was too busy glaring at me.

"That was stupid, Em."

The roar of the crowd was deafening, but I heard each of his words with crystal-clear precision.

I marched toward him. Pete went with me, probably to throw himself in between us if necessary.

"I had it under control," I fumed.

Chase drained the entire bottle of water then tossed it aside. "Yeah. It looked like it with that guy about to make a punching bag out of you."

"It would have been fine."

Chase forced himself to take a deep breath. "That guy was twice your size and didn't seem like the type to have a moral dilemma over taking a swing at a woman."

I pointed out at the stage. "You didn't need to cause a scene."

He blinked at me as though he were trying to determine if I was being serious. "Yeah, because that was all I was thinking about when I intervened. Causing a scene."

His voice was growing, his arms getting animated. His fire fanned the flame building inside me.

"Or maybe it was just another publicity stunt so all your fans can swoon over how chivalrous you are to rip some guy out of a crowd for messing with a woman?" The words exploded out of me, molten hot and piercing.

The skin between his brows creased as he moved away, distancing himself from me. "I'm going to pretend I didn't just hear you say that."

The crowd was still roaring, echoing his name, but I tuned them out. I ignored Dani and her interjections about this not being the time, and I disregarded Pete, who was trying to mediate with one-worded pieces of advice.

"Why? Because it's the truth?" I shouted. "Or

because you don't like someone spelling it out for you like that?"

"I don't want to fight with you right now, and I know from enough experience we're just getting warmed up."

"Why not?" I motioned between the two of us. "Now's as good a time as any to get this all aired out."

His finger stabbed onto the dark stage, sweat still dripping from the ends of his hair and down his face. "I have to go back out there in twenty seconds and sing an encore. Now is not a good time for this."

One of his stagehands slid Chase's guitar back over his head, his bandmates already moving onto the stage under the veil of darkness.

"Fine. Good. You've got a show to finish," I said, moving toward the back stairs.

"Where are you going?"

"The bus." I paused so abruptly, Pete nearly ran into me. My stare cut toward Chase. "Is that okay with you?"

He was already facing the stage, his fingers working the strings of his guitar. "You always do whatever you want. No matter what anyone else's input is."

He loped onto the stage right as the lights blasted on, sending the crowd into a renewed upheaval.

I didn't linger long enough to see which song he'd saved for the encore; I needed air. After thundering down the hall, I shoved through the entry doors and gulped at the night air like I'd been drowning. My hands were still shaking and my vision flashed red, but those were typical reactions to one of Chase's and my fights. We'd known no shortage of them as kids, and I should have known better than to think we'd outgrown it.

Behind me, I heard the music pumping through the stadium, Chase's voice layering on top of the guitar and drums in a way that made a person feel it vibrating inside of their chest.

Pete swung the bus door open, following me as I stormed inside.

"You can head back inside now," I said, kicking off my wedges as though they were the objects of my anger. "I'm sealed up and safe inside this fortress of steel."

Pete clasped his hands in front of him. "I've been instructed to stay with you."

"Your *Chase's* bodyguard."

"I'm Mr. Lawson's employee," he said, staying

planted right where he was. "And I've been instructed that for the entirety of this tour, I am *your* bodyguard. Not to leave you side unless instructed."

"And I just 'instructed' you to leave."

Pete cleared his throat. "Instructed by Mr. Lawson."

My hands curled into fists at my sides. I was supposed to be calming down, not getting into an argument with a guy who outweighed me by a solid two hundred pounds of muscle.

"Not to leave my side?" I repeated. "What if I have to use a public restroom? You going to follow me inside?"

Pete's expression indicated he was arguing with a toddler instead of a full-grown woman. "First, I'd make sure the bathroom was empty. Then I'd temporarily close it off. Finally, yes, I would follow you inside. Because *that's* my job." He lumbered a few steps toward me, seeming to lengthen before my eyes. "And do I seem like the type of guy who doesn't take his job seriously?"

"Think I can handle a five-minute bathroom break on my own," I mumbled.

"Given what I just witnessed inside? Color me skeptical."

My lips pursed. "I had it under control."

"If that was control, I've got a promising future as a horse jockey."

The image of Pete on a racehorse, clinging to stay on top, threatened to unleash a smile. So I took a breath and reminded myself I was upset. "I was fine."

Pete's mouth turned down. "You were. Because Chase stepped in."

My fiery reply was on my lips when the bus door boomed open, followed by thunderous footsteps storming inside. "Pete, I need a few minutes alone with Miss North."

Pete didn't hesitate.

"Never leave my side, eh?" I called after his retreating form.

"*Unless* directed by Mr. Lawson." Pete fired a wink at me before stepping out of the bus, leaving me alone with a man who looked close to his boiling-over point.

Seething or not, I'd never feared Chase. He'd never put his hands on me in that kind of way, no matter how blistering our fights had gotten. He possessed the restraint of a monk where that kind of physical contact was concerned . . . and the restraint of a glutton pertaining to the other type of physicality.

"Here I am." I shattered the silence, swinging out my arms. "Don't hold back."

Instead of popping off whatever it was he was keeping bottled up inside, he bit his tongue, his hands clasped behind his neck as he turned away from me. A frustrated grunt echoed from his chest.

Restraint of a monk, right there.

The back of his shirt was completely soaked in sweat, his hair so wet from the same it looked as though he'd just stepped out of a shower.

Pulling open the fridge, I retrieved a bottle of water. "Here. You're going to need one or twelve of these to rehydrate from the looks of you." I tossed the bottle at him when he was facing me again.

He caught it but set it aside. "The last thing on my mind right now is drinking water."

"What's the first?" I asked, slamming the fridge closed.

"I've got two things in contention for that title." As he stared at me, his eyes were liquid, the way they'd look following a deep kiss or when I put my hands on him.

"Let's see, one of those being scolding me for how stupid I was for what I did out there, and the other being ordering me to remain backstage for every concert from now on?"

His footsteps creaked as he took a few toward me. "One of two you have right."

"The scolding or the ordering?" My hand settled on my hip. "Because you should know from experience I don't respond well to either."

Chase's head fell back, another one of those exasperated sounds rumbling in his chest. "When I tell you to do something, listen."

Lava pumped into my veins. "You did *not* just say that."

Instead of backpedaling, he pushed forward. "Yes, I damn well did." He spoke each word with intention. "The only time I will ever order you to do something is if it has to do with your safety. And that is because I care." Chase's hand went to his chest as he blinked at me like he was waiting for the message to settle in. "Don't blow it off because you have an issue with being told what to do. If I didn't give a shit, I'd save myself the headache and let you do whatever the hell you want. But I do care. A lot. So deal with it."

"You care? A lot?" My voice cracked as tears threatened to breech the surface. I conquered them. "You cared so much for me you left me. Everything we had, everything you promised, you forgot all of it in exchange for a record deal."

A wash of pain crept onto his face. "I was eighteen. I fucked up. I made a mistake I will have to live with for the rest of my life."

I took one look around the lavish tour bus. "Oh yeah. It really looks like you're rotting under the consequences of your choices."

"You really think gaining this is worth all I lost with you?" Chase asked, staring at me exactly how every woman wanted to be looked at by a man at least once in her lifetime.

My anger gave way to something else. "I have no idea. How would I? We haven't so much as texted a happy birthday to each other in ten years." My hand ran through my hair. "How am I supposed to know anything at all other than you left, and *stayed* away, until last week when you approached me with a seven-figure offer for me and a publicity overhaul for you?"

His forehead creased. "The offer? My reputation? Is that what you still think this is all about?"

He allowed the silence to hang between us—as a trap or a tribute, I couldn't tell.

"I know I agreed to six months."

His eyes fell upon me with the kind of impact that forced a cloud of air from my lungs. "And all I know is that you said yes."

He came closer, watching me for any signs of dispute. I had none left to give.

"To what?" The words fell from my lips as his hands settled against the dark window behind me, caging me in with his arms.

His mouth moved toward my ear, his damp cheek dragging against mine. "To me. You said yes to me." The heat of his breath fanned down my neck, the heady scent of him intoxicating my senses. "Say it again."

My head tipped back as his mouth explored the column of my neck, his tongue tasting my skin. "Yes," I breathed, an offering as much as it was a confirmation.

As I said it, he sucked lightly at my neck, but not so carefully that it wouldn't leave a mark. That hadn't changed—his obsession with leaving some mark that claimed me as his. Whether it had been an old sweatshirt, his class ring, or a slight bruise on my neck, Chase took marking his territory seriously.

The air stirred as Chase dropped to his knees before me.

My hands raked through his wet hair as I quirked my eyebrow at him. "What are you doing?"

His hands slid up my legs, disappearing beneath my skirt. "Making up."

He tugged my panties from my hips, slipping them down my legs. He lifted my feet out of them before flinging them aside.

"I think I finally figured out what was on your mind besides yelling at me."

He grinned at me, the one that was part warning in nature, then his head slipped beneath my skirt.

"Chase . . ." I checked the bus door, praying Pete had locked it on his way out.

His name was rising from my lips once more when he rendered me mute. All tension left me as my body seemed to melt under the dexterity of his tongue. His hands spread along the insides of my knees, easing them farther apart.

He kissed me down there in a way that had my nails digging into my palms as though they were out for blood. To save myself the scars, I secured my hands to his shoulders, finding a solid grip as he drew me to the cusp with his intimate kisses.

One of his hands lifted, his fingers dragging along the inside of my thigh. His fingers separated, opening me, his mouth no longer grazing me gently. When my back arched from the window, it released with a wet pop. I was nearly as wet with sweat as he

was, and all it had taken was a few precise place-
ments of his mouth.

His free hand roamed around my hip, digging
into my backside, grinding me against him deeper.
"Tell me when you're close," he husked before
pressing his tongue against me.

I jumped, feeling my release charging to the
surface. "I'm close."

When he sucked me into his mouth, teasing me
with his tongue, my fingers drilled deeper into his
shoulders as my hips flexed against him.

"*So* close," the words drug from my mouth like a
trail of smoke as I felt everything go numb.

Chase's fingers shoved inside me right as I was
on the verge, and the moment I tightened around
him at the crest of my orgasm, he pulled away. His
fingers, mouth, hands—everything.

I stood there, barely able to balance on my own
as I struggled to fill my lungs, my release threat-
ening rebellion. "What are you doing?"

He smoothed my skirt back into place as he rose
to stand before me. His eyes were wild, his pupils
the size of dimes. One corner of his mouth
elevated, his lips glistening from what he'd been
doing to me. "Teaching a lesson."

When my mind cleared enough to grasp the

intention of his meaning, my mouth fell open. "That's low, Lawson. Even for you."

He backed away, his grin spreading as he examined exactly the state he'd put me in and was leaving me in. "I'll make it up to you. Another night."

My damp skin peeled away from the window as I attempted to right myself. My knees were still wobbling from the tremors of my near-orgasm. "You're really going to leave me like this?"

He paused at the door, licking his lips. A rumble rattled low in his throat. "You can take care of yourself, right?" His attempt at an innocent face was an utter failure. He winked at me. "In this circumstance, I'm going to let you."

## 8

"You're staring. Again." I peered across the limo seat at Chase, who was sitting much closer to me than he had been when we'd left the hotel.

"Get used to it," he replied, motioning at me like that was all the explanation I needed.

My eyes met his. "Chase."

"If you're looking for an apology, you're not getting one. You in that dress does not match with apologies." His gaze lingered on the bustline of the dress. Its purpose seemed more slanted toward exposure than coverage.

I tugged at the dress, but it didn't budge. It was as snug as a second skin. "I didn't pick out this dress."

"Then who do I have to thank?"

My eyes lifted in answer at the person across the seat from us.

One of Dani's hands turned over in her lap. "I made a very specific list of items you needed to purchase when I sent you shopping in Nashville. It's not my fault the fanciest dress you returned with was meant for a Governor's Brunch instead of a formal gala." She smiled as she inspected the dress she'd had rushed to the hotel for me earlier today. "You're lucky I've got so many connections at Barney's."

"Spending six hours entombed in this sausage casing is what you consider lucky?"

Dani's tongue worked into her cheek as she went to check something on her phone. "Depends on which side of the dress you're standing."

I fired a dry smile at her, but she wasn't paying attention.

"You look amazing." Chase's hand covered mine twisting in my lap. "And never before has that word felt so inadequate, but goddamn, woman." Chase blew out a breath as his eyes scanned me yet again before shifting his attention to the hulk across from me, beside Dani. "Tall Drink, don't take your eyes off of her tonight, okay?"

My eyes lifted. "Maybe to blink?"

Pete huffed, leaning forward in his seat, staring at me like we were in some kind of staring contest. I cracked first.

"Blinking is overrated," Pete said.

Chase grunted, lifting his hand to high-five Pete.

"Brutes," I mumbled, staring out the window as the limo eased up to the curb outside of the convention center.

Chase let Dani and Pete climb out first, then he pressed himself against me. "I'm looking forward to proving to you exactly how much of a brute I am later tonight." His hand found mine, easing it toward his lap. My stomach flopped when I felt his want in the palm of my hand. "When I rip this dress to shreds to get to your body."

My fingers curled around him, need washing over me, as I leaned in to kiss his neck. "Promises, promises." I planted a kiss just above his collar . . . or maybe partly on it.

When I leaned away, a smile drew on my face when I saw the red mark my lipstick had left behind.

"I'm hard as hell and turned on. How are you expecting me to get out of this limo and survive the next six hours?" He grimaced when my hand released him.

Climbing out of the limo, I reached back for him to take my hand, a playful look on my face. "Follow the breadcrumbs."

His fingers tied through mine as that predator gleam flickered in his eyes.

Pete and Dani were waiting for us on the sidewalk. Her eyes immediately landed on the red lipstick mark splashed across his neck, and she frowned, wiping at his skin with her fingers. She didn't even attempt wiping at the lipstick on his collar. "How's that going to look in photos?"

I aimed my smile at the ground.

"It's going to look like my 'wholesome' country girl on the streets is a sexual deviant in the sheets," Chase teased, holding out his elbow for me to take. "How's that for publicity, Dani?"

"Sexual deviance isn't a difficult attribute to find in women where you're concerned. Wholesomeness, not so much." Dani tried adjusting his tux jacket to cover some of the stain on his shirt, but it didn't work. "Let's remember why we brought her on board, in case the sweat imprints on bus windows, strewn underwear, and lipstick stains were starting to confuse you." She looked between us, lingering on me. "*Both* of you."

Dani's reminder drove deep, the deal struck

between Chase and me wedging between us as we turned to head up the stairs riddled with photographers and fans, all thrashing at the rail barriers as though they'd all taken rabid.

Chase didn't have a response. Instead, he led me up the red-carpet-lined stairs, where my arm wove through his. "Nervous?" he whispered, tipping his head up at the cameras, already flashing at us like a million tiny strobes.

My throat moved. "I'm fine." I formed a smile and held it in place as we made our entrance.

Chase was an old pro, pausing when we made it to each landing, waving, smiling, angling us so every camera had a good shot. This was the Chase who was a stranger to me, the one who abided paparazzi and indulged simpering fans. It was so contrary to the hot-headed boy who didn't do anything unless he damn well wanted to I'd fallen in love with years ago. A part of me respected his honed skill at working a crowd, yet another part mourned the boy who didn't give a shit what anyone thought of him.

It took us almost twenty minutes before we made it inside. I was exhausted and I hadn't stepped foot into the gala itself.

"Did Dani prep you on what this is all about

tonight?" Chase drew me closer, heading toward the ballroom.

My head moved as I struggled to blink the phantom camera flashes from my vision. "This is a benefit gala for a local children's hospital that doesn't require payment from families who are unable to provide it," I said, reciting lines from the drawn-out spiel Dani had given over lunch earlier. "You're the honorary guest, roughly three thousand of Houston's elite will also be in attendance, there'll be hor d'ouerves, drinks, dancing, I'm to stay close if you need me but not so close as to come off as clingy. You'll be busy posing for photos, signing autographs, and humoring, though not indulging, a likely drove of female admirers." I could sense the amused look on his face. "According to Dani, of course. Because I'm not so sure you could make a lonely widow blush if you stripped down to your skivvies and gave her a lap dance these days. Your heart throb days are a good five years behind you, Chase Lawson."

His hand gripped a solid handful of my ass right before we stepped inside the ballroom. "We'll see who I can make blush tonight."

Everyone in the room clapped in response to his appearance. I stood there, at his side, taking in the scene, wondering where I fit in. Not with the social elite who reeked of advantage and wealth. Not with Chase's team milling into the room behind us, knowing exactly what to say and do at the right time.

With Chase?

Maybe at one point in our lives that was where I fit, but the grooves and cuts no longer fit. Life and experience had reshaped us, so our jagged edges no longer fit together as seamlessly as before.

Dani wasted no time steering us toward an older man who possessed the kind of eyes that oozed privilege. "Chase, I'd like to introduce you to Ted Warner, the owner and CEO of KBLM Houston."

While Chase was distracted, I seized the opportunity to slip away.

Of course, my shadow floated one and a half steps behind me.

"I'm fine," I chimed, glancing at Pete over my shoulder.

"I'm here. Of course you are." Pete was in his standard black, though tonight's outfit was a suit that looked as though it had been tailored with Zeus in mind.

"Hey, I've been meaning to ask you." I plucked

a couple of coconut shrimp from a server's tray as we passed. Probably not a good idea to eat since I could barely breathe in my dress, but I was starving. "Do you carry a gun?"

That drew a sharp laugh from Pete. "Do I look like I need a gun?"

"Good point." I patted his chest, which was the equivalent of an armored vehicle. "You're pretty much a walking grenade launcher."

"Pretty much," he echoed, shaking his head when I offered him the second shrimp. "I don't eat on the job."

"On the job?" I glanced around, focusing on all of the threats in their diamond necklaces and platinum cufflinks. "What do you think is going to happen?"

"Nothing," Pete answered succinctly. "Because I'm *on the job*."

Waving him off, I stuffed the other shrimp in my mouth, embellishing the sound of enjoyment I gave as I ate it.

After that, I rotated around the room, sneaking an appetizer or two whenever the trays passed, nursing a glass of champagne, and repressing my inner rage whenever I noticed the latest young, gushing beauty dangling off of

Chase like an annoying hangnail I wanted to rip off.

"It's part of the job, you know." Pete tipped his head in the direction I was looking. Where Chase just so happened to be . . . along with a redhead who was all legs and tits.

"Sure, it is," I muttered into my champagne glass. "Putting up with beautiful, wealthy woman who would pretty much do anything to claim a share in the Chase Lawson record book is a real hardship."

As if able to hear me from way across the room, Chase's gaze drifted from his present ingénue to land on me. He gave me one of those looks that said a million things with one private exchange. I tipped my glass at him, diverting my attention.

"For some men, fame is a blessing." Pete hinted at what he was suggesting as he stared at the cluster of woman circling Chase. "For some, it's a curse."

"Sell your psychology to someone else, Dr. Pete. I'm not buying any more crazy this lifetime." I nudged him before turning to leave the room.

"Where are you going?" he asked, on my heels.

"Somewhere you're not allowed."

"I go where you go. That's *where* I'm allowed."

Out in the hallway, I clucked my tongue at the

women's restroom door. "No dicks allowed." Flashing an evil smile, I ducked inside the bathroom before he could argue.

My solitude didn't last long. A hulking figure shoved through the bathroom door, his expression reading *That all you got?*

"Excuse me?" Pete's voice boomed through the women's bathroom. "Is there anyone else in here?"

I crouched to look under the stalls, praying I'd find a few sets of heels. My luck had always run in short supply.

Pete smirked at me, crossing his arms as he stationed himself at the doorway. He motioned at the line of stalls. "Your move."

My glare wasn't very impressive as I stomped into the farthest stall. "This is humiliating, you know that?"

"Your pride is a small price to pay in exchange for your safety."

A huff of protest bled from my mouth as I wrestled with my dress to get it up and out of the way. With all of the beadwork, by the time I had it gathered far enough above my waist to do my business, I felt like I was clutching twenty pounds in my arms.

"I've got stage fright," I called out after a minute, my heels tapping impatiently.

Pete sighed, his footsteps ringing through the bathroom. The sound of a faucet cranking on followed. "Better?"

I relaxed. Finally. "Thank you."

"See? Even *my* pride's a small price to pay in exchange for your safety," Pete grumbled.

The door whipped open, followed by a surprised, distinctly female, gasp.

"Excuse me, ma'am. The restroom will be reopened in just a moment." Pete's voice was all deep and creamy, just enough authority in it to compel compliance.

When I emerged from the stall, my head shook as I went to wash my hands at the faucet that was still running. "You should get a raise."

"If you keep proving to be this difficult, I'm going to request one."

While I deposited my hand towel in the hamper, Pete swung the door open for me. "I'll ease up. Now that you've proven you literally have no boundaries."

Leaving the women's restroom, I made sure to smile brightly at the women outside, blinking between Pete and me like we were a hot headline just waiting to happen.

"What do people do for fun at these things?" I

blew out a breath when I stepped back into the ball-room, finding it exactly as thrilling as I'd left it. The leggy redhead had been replaced by an exotic-looking brunette with an ass that couldn't have been crafted without the aid of implants.

"Hell if I know," Pete grunted.

Doing another scan, this one more inclusive instead of so focused on Chase, I noticed a couple tables tucked toward the back of the room. A group of children and adults I guessed were their parents were seated there. A couple kids were in wheel-chairs, a few had prosthetics, and more than seemed fair had the sallow pallor and sunken hollows of what could only be cancer's ire.

I started in that direction, holding up the next server I passed balancing a tray of desserts on their hand. Not saying a word, I took the tray and proceeded toward the back of the ballroom.

"Who's hungry for some dessert?" I asked as I held out the tray of treats between the two tables.

The kids didn't jump at the dessert offer quite like I'd planned. Some of the parents looked between each other.

"That's a thoughtful gesture," one of the moms said, pointing at a cart that was rolling closer. From what I could see, it looked like it was an ice cream cart with just about every topping imaginable available. "Mr. Lawson ordered a special dessert just for the kids."

"Oh." Glimpsing between my basic dessert options and the Mecca of ice cream sundaes, I accepted that to an eight-year-old, crème brulee sucked compared to a triple waffle cone with gummy worms piled on top. I handed the giant tray to Pete. "Here. Eat something. You're looking thin."

He gave his standard head shake, the one that was parental in nature, before passing the tray off to the next server who whisked by.

"You're Mr. Lawson's girlfriend." One of the young girls giggled, pointing at the assortment of toppings she wanted to accompany her bowl of bubblegum ice cream.

"So I'm told." I smiled, lifting my hand to my mouth as though I were about to disclose a secret. "Which means I can totally round up some autographed souvenirs if anyone's a Chase Lawson fan here."

The kids exploded over that, a dozen mouths sputtering on about Chase this and Chase that as though he were the best thing since sour gummies.

"So what should I round up? Shirts? Hats?" I fired a wink. "Both?"

The same mom who'd broke the news to me about the ice cream cart had that same look of discomfort on her face again. I was about to inquire as to why every adult at those two tables looked like they had a bad case of indigestion when one of the boys lifted a large bag.

"Mr. Lawson dropped these souvenir bags off for us earlier," he said, pulling items out one at a time. "He signed them all too."

Hats, shirts, sweatshirts, posters . . . a damn blanket. He'd hooked those kids up.

"*And* we all got a trip to Disneyland with our families from Mr. Lawson too," another boy blurted before shoving a spoonful of whipped cream and cherries into his mouth.

I made sure my excitement matched theirs. "Disneyland? Lucky!"

"All expenses paid, five star all the way." One of the moms squeezed my arm. "Please thank him again for us. A trip like that is something our family could never have managed on our own."

I had to swallow the ball in my throat before I could reply. "I'll tell him."

Waving goodbye to everyone, I started to leave, but a small hand slipped into mine. The little girl touching me was beaming up at me, holding out a bowl of chocolate ice cream with just about every topping available. "For you."

"Now *that's* a dessert." I gave her a side hug after taking the bowl. "Thank you."

A chorus of goodbyes followed me as I left, Pete settling in beside me.

"Miss North!" a voice chimed from off to the side.

"Journalist. Don't stop," Pete instructed under his voice.

When the woman called my name once more, practically barreling in front of my path, I broke to a stop.

Pete gave me a look.

"I can handle it," I whispered to him.

His look deepened.

"Miss North. Jenny Hutchins, KNBC News." Her fake smile hiccupped when she noticed the three and a half pounds of dessert I was carrying. "I was wondering if I could ask you a few questions."

Pete cleared his throat.

I stood up straighter. "A few."

"You and Chase go way back," she started, as though she'd memorized her lines weeks ago.

I remembered what Dani had taught me about

interacting with the media: don't say the first thing that comes to your mind, and keep your answers as short and vague as possible. "We learned to ride bikes together, so yeah, we've known each other for quite a while."

"You were lovers too?" When I remained quiet, she glanced at me through her reading glasses.

"Boyfriend and girlfriend."

"What did you think when you heard about the accident?" she asked, gauging my reaction from my eyes to my posture to my hands. "Did he drink a lot back then too?"

Beside me, Pete was clearly growing impatient, but I could handle this. There was no way to avoid the media for the next six months, given who Chase was and the hot topics pinned to him, and tonight was as good a night as any to get my first encounter over with.

"No." My hands tied together to keep them from fidgeting. "I was surprised."

"He claims he doesn't drink anymore." The reporter glanced at Chase with what looked to be a glass of water or sparkling water in his hand. Then she leaned in, bestowing an ambiguous smile upon me. "But come on, girl to girl, what else is sloshing around in that glass when the camera's turn off?"

I leaned away, feeling a strong stab of protec-
tiveness for Chase. "Nothing."

The reporter studied me for a minute, looking
for a crack to break. She gave a chuckle as she
shrugged. "You're a good liar," she said as though
she were giving a compliment. "But you have to
become one when a loved one has a drinking problem, don't you?"

Heat flooded my face from this woman and her
accusations. She was calling Chase a drunk and me
a liar. He might have had drinking issues, but he'd
put those behind him. I might have lied for him
before, and I would again, but I wasn't now.

"Those few questions are up." I pointed my
spoon at her before digging it into the melting pile
of ice cream and taking a massive bite.

Leaving her, I inspected the room, still unsure
where I fit into this foreign puzzle. All I wanted to
do was relax in a quiet room and eat my ice cream.
I couldn't take one more stilted conversation or hold
the precise angle of a smile for one more minute.

"Ma'am?" Pete's voice sounded almost uncer-
tain. "Are you okay?"

"Please, for the love of all things good and true,
stop calling me ma'am. My name is Emma. Or Em
if you're thinking we'll be friends after all of this is

over." I waved my finger at Pete as we kept marching out of that ballroom. "And if one more person asks me if I'm okay, I'm going to lose it."

Pete's brows pinched together. "So does that mean you are okay or are not okay?" He must have felt my rage, because he quickly added, "Emma? Em."

I plucked one of the maraschino cherries from the mountain of whipped cream and popped it into my mouth. "It means I am or will soon be okay."

As I wove down the hallway, something caught my eye. A perfect hiding spot.

The woman working the coatroom gave me a funny look when I dodged inside, but she didn't put up any protest. I figured as long as I didn't spill ice cream on the fur coats, she didn't care how long I hid out. Pete didn't follow me inside, but I knew he'd perched himself right outside the door. I guessed he figured there were more potential threats lurking in a women's bathroom than a musty coatroom.

Leaning into a wall, I slithered down to the floor, hearing the seams of my dress stretching. The sturdy stitching might have survived the night thus far, but it would not outlast the ice cream. Or the two dozen toppings piled on top.

Eating my stress away, I finally relaxed now that I'd found a quiet, private space. God, I was bad at this. My first public appearance with Chase and I'd barely made it four hours before breaking down into an exhausted mess.

Names to remember, a thousand cameras, mind-numbing conversations, keeping up airs and personifying perfection . . . this was not the world I'd grown up in, nor the life I wanted.

I'd nearly made it to the bottom of the bowl when I forced myself to set it aside. I'd achieved glutton status ten bites earlier.

"Mind if I hide out in here for a while too?" A familiar figure crept in past the door, sealing it closed behind him.

"I guess I can share my coat closet." I scooted aside to make room for him.

"I see you found the ice cream cart." Chase eyed the nearly empty bowl when he came to a stop in front of me.

My arms rung around my stomach. "You're really sending all of those kids to Disneyland?"

"You gotta spend your money on something, because you can't take it with you."

"But you can leave behind a legacy. Have a building named for you. Or a monument."

His eyes squinted. "Pretty positive those kids are going to enjoy Disneyland infinitely more than anyone who passed by a monument of yours truly."

My head tipped back to look up at him. "You're a good person, Chase Lawson."

His boot tapped my foot. "Picked it up by following someone else's example."

A sound of protest rattled in my chest. "I thought I was being all awesome by offering them two-by-two-inch desserts and autographed ball caps. You ordered up the damn ice cream man and an all-expense paid trip to a kid's paradise."

"You give what you can with what you've got." Chase's brow lifted as he quoted one of my mom's old sayings. "Some of us just have more to give."

I nodded, glancing at the door. "You want to get out of here?"

"Like . . . leave?"

"Not like it. Exactly like it." When I started to stand, he held out his hand for me to take. "Let's leave."

Chase exhaled as he pulled me up. "I can't."

"Of course you can. You're a grown man."

"No, Em. I can't." His head lowered to align with mine. "I'm the special guest listed for this benefit, which means I can't just bail because I feel like it."

"You've done your time," I said, hating the hint of a whine I detected in my voice.

"It's part of the job." His thumb wiped the corner of my mouth as he fought a smile. I probably had dried ice cream staining the lower half of my face. "There are parts I don't like, but that comes with anything. You take the good with the bad. Just make sure the good's worth it."

I stared at the racks of coats, feeling embarrassed. I could operate a combine and could fix a fence pole in five minutes flat—I was not the type to retreat when life got hard. "When did you become so responsible?"

"It was more of a byproduct than a choice." His thumb dragged across my lips before he backed away. "I've got a couple more hours to soldier through, but you can head back to the hotel with Pete if you want. Unless you like the company of leather and tweed." He pinched one of the jackets as he passed, seeming amused by the image of me in my fancy dress, hiding out in a closet full of coats, an abandoned ice cream bowl nearby.

Licking my lips to remove any leftover ice cream

bits, I smoothed my dress and slipped back into my heels. "I'll go with you."

He blinked as though he'd heard me wrong.

My shoulder lifted. "You're not the only one who has a job to do. I signed on for a six-month contract, and by god, even if these people suck the will to live right out of me, I'm not disappearing again."

"Em, you've made your appearance, posed for the photos. You can leave. I'm not paying you a million bucks to suffer through every grueling minute of one of these things at my side."

I stopped in front of him. "Then why are you paying me?"

His expression drew together as he considered how to best put his words.

"Exactly. If you give me free passes to these public things, then the only services you're paying me for are the ones shared in private. And that makes me feel like some call girl or something dirty like that."

"If that were true, and I really could just call on you whenever I had an urge . . ." His eyes darkened as they skimmed down me. "Everything I've got, it's all yours."

I snapped in front of his face to try to clear the

devilish slant of his expression. No dice. "You'd give up everything you own—every car, house, investment, jet, et cetera—for six months of whenever, wherever sex?"

One brow disappeared into his hairline. "*However* included in that sex clause?"

"Why not."

Chase followed me as I pushed through the coatroom door. "I would give up everything for *one week* of that kind of sex with you."

My back tingled from the way his hand glided around my back, finding its home on the bend of my waist. However, I made sure to give him my most unimpressed look. "So much for that responsibility byproduct we were just talking about."

"I'm responsible." He waved at Pete when we steered down the hall, moving toward the ballroom. "But I also happen to know the value of good sex."

"Something tells me you haven't been hurting in the sex department." I eyed the cluster of women inside the ballroom, regarding Chase as though he were a deity they'd willingly sacrifice their firstborn for.

Chase pulled me closer, his face tipping toward mine. "You're the only good I've ever had, Emma North."

More chills, these kind spilling down my arms as well.

Around the ballroom, I noticed the number of phones and cameras aiming our way, documenting the tarnished golden boy attempting to polish up his reputation with his small-town high school sweetheart.

"Two more hours? You got this?" he asked, giving me a way out.

"You have to take the bad with the good. Just make sure the good's worth it."

The corners of his eyes creased. "Does that mean what I think it does?"

"It means I'm still trying to figure it out."

## 9

It was the fifth concert in the tour and we were in Charlotte. No, Charleston. I was getting my Carolinas confused, which was a direct result of spending the last day and a half on the road.

The rock star lifestyle, at least the way Chase did it, was not the least bit glamorous. Instead of empty alcohol bottles, it was sparkling water and green juice that smelled like manure and fresh-cut grass. Instead of lines of cocaine, it was a multi-vitamin schedule that damn near required a flow chart to execute. Instead of a steady stream of groupies rotating through the bus, there was me, with my messy ponytail and faded jeans, and occasionally Dani, with her stiff suits and legion of techy devices.

I'd spent the afternoon and evening exploring the city and arrived back in time for the last couple of songs. Pete and I were bobbing our heads backstage as Chase and his band ripped out the final chorus to "Lead Me On." Dani posed with a towel and bottle of water. I'd already settled into something of a routine, though I doubted I'd ever get used to the flashing cameras and shouts whenever Chase and I went anywhere in public.

The stage went dark, followed by five figures loping offstage. The roar of the crowd amplified and would continue its assault until the band made its reappearance for the encore in three minutes, give or take a few seconds depending on how urgent Dani was with her shoves and chides.

Chase took the water bottle but not the towel. He dumped the entire contents over his head, coming straight toward me with a flicker in his eye. Before I could register it, his hand grabbed mine, pulling me deeper backstage with him.

"No one gets by," he said to Pete, who barricaded himself in front of us with a look on his face that suggested he hoped someone tried.

"Chase?" I shouted above the deafening cheers, having to jog to keep up with him.

He didn't stop or reply. Not until we were

tucked away toward the back of the stage, cloistered in by dark curtains and excess stage equipment.

His hands gripped into my hips before lifting me onto a backup speaker. He pulled me to the very end of it, so I was barely teetering on the edge.

"What are you doing?" I asked, my heart hammering, not sure if he was suffering from heat-stroke or some other ailment.

His mouth dropped to my neck, sucking at it urgently. "You," he husked as he unzipped his fly.

A bolt of energy shot up my spine. "You've got to be back on stage in two minutes." I gasped when he yanked my panties aside, pushing my legs open when he stepped closer.

"All I need's a minute." His hand wound behind my neck, his other dropping to my hip, bracing himself . . .

My gasp echoed from my lips, tangling with his own cries of pleasure as he moved inside me, his need desperate, urgent, as though I was all that stood between him and death. His head dropped beside mine as he rutted against me, the sounds he was making more primal than man.

"Let me feel you," he demanded, his grip tightening behind my neck. "Let me feel you come all over me."

My body seemed tuned to his bidding, servient to his commands. My head fell back as my release rushed through me, the rest of my body following, but Chase caught my fall, holding me close as I felt the earth opening up to swallow me.

"God damn," he grunted, as his body stiffened against mine, his dick burying deep as he spent his release inside me.

He stood there for a moment, trembling in my arms, as I tried to catch up to what had just happened. Slowly, one piece at a time, reality swept in around us again.

The roar of the crowd broke through my shell first. "You've got an encore to play," I breathed against his neck, loving the way his sweat felt against my skin.

"I'm not sure I could play a basic C chord in this state." His voice was deeper than normal, gravelly from sex.

"No warning, no foreplay, you made me come in a whole sixty seconds." My hand lowered to where our bodies were still joined, palming his balls. A shudder ripped through him. "You can damn well fly if you put your mind to it."

His eyes dropped to our locked bodies, his jaw setting as a grunt rumbled in his chest.

From the other side of the curtain, we both heard Pete's unmistakable clearing of a throat. "Mr. Lawson."

Chase groaned, pressing his lips to mine as he slid out of me. He chuckled softly when he felt my lips turn down. "Two more songs, then we've got all night, Em."

"You finally decided to fuck me with something other than your mouth?"

"Finally? Are you sure that's the word you want to use?" His eyes fired with a challenge.

I leaned closer. "I'm sure."

After tucking himself into his pants, he snapped my panties back into place. "You know I love when you underestimate me." He kissed my neck before backing away. "It's when I'm at my best."

I gestured at myself, still shaking, my chest moving like I was suffocating, the remnants of our lovemaking winding down my thighs. "I think you proved your point."

One side of his mouth lifted as he started to duck outside of the curtain. "You good?"

I lifted my thumb. "Understatement." As he slid past the curtain, going to answer the rumble of his fans, I called, "Five months and ten more days."

I knew he heard me, I knew it, but he didn't reply.

ANOTHER CONCERT. ANOTHER CITY. I WAS losing track, but I knew we were somewhere in California.

We were in the bus on the way to a hotel after the concert. Chase didn't have a concert tomorrow night, which meant we didn't need to hit the road to race to the next city.

Chase was in the back, showering and changing, while I sat at the table with Pete and Dani, all of us sipping chamomile tea. As I'd mentioned, this was a wild bunch.

"Tomorrow Chase has a golf event at the Coast Inn Country Club. Should I mark you down as a player or spectator, Emma?" Dani paused long enough to look up at me from her laptop. The icy storm front had somewhat abated where I was concerned, but she still talked to me like she was explaining a playground slide to an adolescent.

"Eh, can I call dibs on driving the cart?" I asked.

Dani gave one of her quiet sighs as she finished her email. "I'll make the request."

Pulling out my phone, I found I'd missed a few messages from friends and family back home. Between their calls and my own, I spoke to my parents daily. It was the same with my friends. If it wasn't Jesse checking in to see how I was dealing with the whole Chase situation, it was Brooke gushing about the dress she'd seen me wearing in whatever tabloid or online article she'd recently been stalking. Sophia was always the one to let me know I was missed and that everyone couldn't wait to see me again soon.

I missed home. But getting to see the country, even in fleeting rushes through bus windows, was exhilarating. Getting to experience it all with Chase made it that much better.

"Fresh and clean." A billow of steam followed Chase as he emerged from the back rooms, tugging on a light T-shirt.

"Good timing. We're just rolling up." Dani shut off her myriad of devices, tucking them safely away in her sleek leather briefcase.

Pete chugged the rest of his tea as he slid out of his seat.

"You clean up nicely," I said.

His mouth quirked. "And you dirty up nicely."

Dani cleared her throat, moving toward the front of the bus.

I held out what was left of my tea, but he grabbed a bottle of water instead. "Gotta stay hydrated." He bounced his brows at me as he drained half the bottle. "It's gonna be a long night."

I patted his chest as I moved by. "You've been going off of four hours of sleep for the last week. You need sleep, not sex."

He choked on his sip of water. "Blasphemy."

I shook my head. "Your libido still thinks it's 2008."

His arms rung around my waist. "My libido is immune to time's march, thank you very much."

I wiggled my butt against his "libido" physically manifesting. We adjusted our positioning before stepping off the bus, the usual collection of photographers, journalists, and fans assembled outside the hotel no matter how hard Dani tried to keep Chase's schedule private.

"Smile and wave," I rattled off, more to myself than to Chase. He was a natural when it came to captivating a crowd.

"Chase!" One voice sounded above the crowd's babble. "Chase Lawson!" The same voice, louder still.

A woman off to our right caught my attention. The way she was leaping into the air, her expression a different tenor than the rest, alerted me this wasn't the average fan.

I nudged Chase as we continued toward the hotel, Pete and a few other guards maintaining a tight circle around us. "Do you know her?" I asked him, pointing at her with my eyes.

Chase gave her a quick inspection. "Nope."

That only sufficed to intensify her shouts and frantic movements as she fought through the wave of bodies to stay positioned beside us.

"She seems to know you."

"There's one in every city." Chase tucked his arm around me when the crowd squeezed in, almost draping himself around me.

"A fan who'd commit murder in exchange for a strand of your golden hair?" I teased.

"For lack of a better analogy, yes." He evaded a cameraman who'd charged into our path.

Dani was waiting just inside the hotel doors with a host of hotel and tour security. We only needed to make it a few more meters and we'd be in the clear.

"Chase Dean Lawson!" From out of nowhere, that girl lunged in front of us, holding out her hands when security pressed in on her. "I have to talk to you."

The surprise of it stopped Chase and me in our tracks. She couldn't have been much taller than me and had managed to successfully halt a herd of heavily muscled guards.

Chase waved Pete and one of the other guys aside. "Say what you need to say," he said to the woman.

Her doe-like eyes circled the spectacle around us. "In private."

My body tensed while Chase's seemed to relax. He might have been used to those kinds of super fans, but I was not.

"Whatever you need to say to me, you can say right here," he said, shaking his head at Dani, who was animatedly slashing her hand across her throat.

She scanned the crowd again, biting her lip as her eyes dropped to the ground.

The alerts were firing inside me; something was wrong. I knew that before she sucked in the breath and lifted her gaze to meet Chase's.

"I'm the mother of your child."

## 10

WE'D SLEPT IN SEPARATE ROOMS LAST NIGHT. AT my request. Chase didn't even try to talk me out of it.

Pete remained stationed outside my hotel room throughout the night, occasionally checking in to see if I needed anything. I only needed one thing —answers.

After the shock of last night, I guessed it was a sleepless night for all of us. I'd heard Dani in the room next to me, on the phone all night, running crisis management with Chase's PR team as the news spread like wildfire about the woman claiming to be the mother of Chase Lawson's child. For once, I felt sorry for Dani.

When the sun cracked through my window the

next morning, I felt numb. Not so much from the possibility that Chase had a child with another woman, but that I'd let myself get so carried away in the fantasy of him and me, the illusion that there was no one else who'd been in his life in that decade we'd spent apart.

A knock at my door a little before eight in the morning stirred me from my broodings. I was expecting anyone besides who I found on the other side of the door.

Chase didn't just look like he hadn't slept; he looked like he'd taken a side trip to hell. He was in the same clothes he'd bounced off the bus in, his eyes dark, and his posture slack.

"I don't know what to say right now." I slumped into the doorway, rubbing at the tie of my bathrobe.

"I know exactly what to say." When I shook my head, he interrupted. "You don't have to say a word. You can get back to ignoring me once I say what I need to if you want, I promise."

"I'm not trying to hurt or punish you. I just need some time."

His hands tucked into his front pockets. "You can have all the time you want. Just, please, let me explain my side of the story first."

That throb in my chest ached from seeing him

like this, hearing the pain in his voice. I stepped aside, letting him into my room. "Okay."

"Not here." A small light flickered in his muted eyes. "Can you be ready to leave in a half hour?"

"Leave to go where?"

"Somewhere," he replied, already backing down the hall toward his room. "Just you and me. No one else."

My eyes cut to Pete, my devoted shadow who could smash a car with his forehead.

"Not even him," Chase added.

"In public?"

Chase gave a non-committal head tip.

"That sounds dangerous."

"You'll be with me." His wide shoulders lifted. "You'll be perfectly safe."

I watched him duck into his room, knowing that the biggest danger I faced was my feelings for Chase.

It only took me twenty minutes to get ready, so I passed the last ten texting my mom, who could tell something was wrong from the tone of my texts. I played it off by explaining the tour was exhausting and I was probably catching a cold, but she didn't buy it. Where Chase was concerned, Mom always defaulted to skeptical.

Collecting my things when I heard the next knock, I steeled myself for whatever he had to say. I'd come into this agreement despising Chase, and I'd let myself get sucked into the glamour of the whole arrangement. Chase had left me for this gig, he'd stayed away for ten years, and we'd only reconnected because he was looking to tidy up his tainted reputation. I was a means to an end.

He was a means to an end for me too.

He smiled when he took me in after I opened the door. "Perfect. You dressed for the occasion."

I inspected my cut-offs and button-down plaid shirt, finished off with my favorite boots and ball cap. "What's the occasion?"

He indicated at himself in the most relaxed, worn-in jeans I'd seem him in and boots that looked like they were nearing their expiration point. "Being us."

My forehead creased.

"Hey, would you mind letting me borrow one of those trucker hats you love so much?"

The folds in my forehead deepened. "You hate those things."

"No, I *hate* them on me. I love them on you." He pinched the bill of my hat, giving it a light shake.

"Then why do you want to borrow one?" I asked, even as I headed toward my suitcase to retrieve a backup.

"For reasons." His smile had grown by the time I made my way back with the extra hat.

Mine debuted when he noticed the color of it, accompanied by the logo.

"Would these reasons have anything to do with you dressing like the rest of us mere mortals?" I asked as I settled the hat on his head.

I choked on the laugh rising inside. Pete couldn't contain his though. Chase's head was not made for trucker hats.

"Possibly." Chase clapped his hand over Pete's shoulder when the two of us moved toward the elevator.

From the set of Pete's jaw, it was as though he was being asked to watch his mother be murdered before his eyes.

"Is that also why you've got those Top Gun sunglasses hanging from your shirt?" I continued as we climbed onto the elevator.

"What? Did you expect me to go out in public without at least trying to disguise myself a little?" Chase dropped the sunglasses into place before the elevator doors chimed open on the first floor. "I might make my share of mistakes, but I'm not stupid."

He nudged me, holding out another pair of sunglasses. I reached into my purse and flashed my own pair of sunglasses at him before slipping them on. "Neither am I."

He chuckled, trying to be discreet as he scanned the lobby. Just your usual hotel guests and employees milling about, though out front was a different story. The number of cameras had tripled from last night, thanks to the news that had gone viral about Chase Lawson's love child.

The reminder had my stomach roiling for the thousandth time since those words had come from that young woman's mouth.

"This way." Taking my hand, Chase led the way down a hall. He shoved open a door that appeared to be an employee entrance.

"Are you going to tell me where we're going yet?" I asked when we paused so Chase could check the back parking lot before leading us into it.

"Nope."

"Why not?" Our boots clapped across the pavement toward the street. Was he heading toward a bus stop?

"Because I want it to be a surprise. You always

loved surprises." When we came within a few meters of the bus stop, he slowed, still casually scanning the area for anyone who might have recognized us.

"I'm starting to rethink my stance on surprises after last night," I muttered as a city bus sputtered up to the curb in front of us.

Chase sighed as he dug out some money for the fare. "This is a good surprise."

"What? Finding out you have a child you didn't know about wasn't a good one?" I could taste the bitterness in my tone on the tip of my tongue.

"We'll talk about that when we get there."

"When we get *where*?" I asked as I trudged onto the bus with him.

Chase paid the fare as though he'd done it a million times, though I couldn't imagine public transportation was a frequent means of getting around for someone like him.

"A city bus?" I said, twisting around in my seat once we'd settled in, taking in the scene. "This was your ideal locale for explaining everything to me?"

"I like city buses. I've written plenty of songs riding one of these."

"What do you like about them?"

"They remind me of who I am. Where I came from. What I want." Chase settled deeper into his seat, as though he were as home in the cracked vinyl as he was in his personal tour bus. "When you strip away everything that isn't real, you're forced to confront the person you really are."

"Public transportation really does bring out the sentiment in you." I tried relaxing into my seat the same way, but I couldn't. It must have been an acquired taste.

We rode in silence after that, staring out the window and taking in the different kinds of people filing on and off the bus.

"Didn't you have a golf thing this morning?" I remembered when Chase nudged me at the next stop.

"I did. But Dani worked her magic and got me out of it." He followed me into the aisle as we departed the bus.

"I bet it drives her insane when you cancel something." I could picture Dani's face all red as she pounded at her laptop, adjusting the schedule.

"I've never had to cancel anything before. This is a first, and I'm sure she can manage."

"You've never cancelled something like that golf

or benefit thing before?" I paused on the sidewalk, no idea where we were or where we were heading.

"Nope." His head shook once.

"Then why start today?"

"Because this is important."

I fell in beside him when he started down the sidewalk buzzing with bodies. "Explaining what happened last night was more important than some golf fundraiser thing?"

He ignored the tint of sarcasm in my voice. "You. *You're* more important than that. Or anything else."

We stopped at a crosswalk, waiting for the light to turn. "Oh."

Chase leaned in. "And that golf thing was a fundraiser to send some local rich kid on the pro circuit. Pretty sure the fellow rich golfers don't need my help to make that happen."

I jogged through the crosswalk with him, finally noticing where we were. My feet froze the moment they came in contact with the walkway running parallel to the beach. "The ocean."

Chase eased me forward a little, moving us out of the way of the steady stream of runners, cyclists, and skateboarders. "Takes your breath away, doesn't it?"

I breathed in the salty air, soaking in the chorus of the waves crashing into the beach beyond us. The dark blue speckled with orbs of silver from the sunlight above, the gentle breeze playing with the ends of my hair. All I could do was nod.

"Come on." He turned down the sidewalk, waiting for me. "There's a better view up here."

A short walk revealed a massive pier jutting out into the ocean, and what looked to be a scaled-down version of an amusement park was situated on top. Early as it was in the day, swarms of people were roaming on and off the pier.

"Of all the places you could go, of all the ways you can get there . . ." I surveyed the scene as we crossed onto the massive pier. "You choose a city bus and a public place like this?"

Chase adjusted his hat a tad lower, his sunglasses having been shielding his eyes since we left the elevator at the hotel. "It seemed like the kind of place you'd like. You always loved the county fair every summer, and I think this is the coastal California equivalent."

I smiled when I noticed the endless food options, reveling in the scent of deep-fried you-name-it. "I mainly loved sampling my way through as many food stands as possible. And riding the rides. Oh, and playing the games."

Chase pulled out his wallet when he noticed the elephant ear vendor up ahead. "And petting every animal that would let you, *and* examining every flower entry, *and* posing in every wood cutout for a picture." Chase lifted one finger at the employee, handing him a twenty.

"And *you* always hated the county fair."

"I might have hated going with school or with my friends, but I loved going with you." Chase handed me the warm elephant ear while the employee made change.

I did a slow spin, my smile growing with every game, ride, and flashing sign I saw. "What's not to love?"

Behind his sunglasses, I could just make out his eyes softening as he stared at me. "Absolutely nothing."

I tore off a chunk of the elephant ear as a distraction while the employee handed Chase his change. Chase took it and stuffed the extra fifteen bucks in the tip jar.

"What do you want to do first?"

"Done." I held up my treat before tearing another chunk off for him.

He frowned. "No thanks."

My gaze latched onto his forearms, looking ever so muscled and fine. "I'm sure they'll have a protein shake and kale chip stand just up ahead. But if they don't—"

This time when I held out the piece, he opened his mouth and let me stuff it in. "God, that's good."

"Flour, cinnamon, sugar, and fryer oil is always good." I licked my fingers as we wandered down the bustling pier. "But there goes your eight-pack. Sorry."

When I held up the next piece, he didn't even hesitate.

"Eight-packs are so last summer." He grinned at me as he chewed.

That image of him was so similar to the teenage version I'd fallen for, I experienced that giddy, lovesick sensation I'd spent two years drowning in.

"Now that we've crossed number one off on your list, what do you want to do *now*?" Chase angled us toward one of my favorite games—the balloon pop—but I held my line leading toward the end of the pier.

"I want to talk," I said, not needing to say anything else for him to understand.

The grin vanished from his face. "Sure you

don't want to put yourself into a little more of a food coma before we have that talk?"

"I'm sure." The next bite I took didn't taste like anything at all.

Chase and I walked the rest of the pier in silence. The squawk of gulls, the waves beating the pillars, and the cacophony of noise from the rides filled the quiet for us.

I still had half of my elephant ear left when we reached the end, but my stomach wouldn't tolerate another morsel. The crowd had thinned out since the amusements ended several meters back, so there was just enough privacy to bridge a delicate topic.

Chase didn't seem to know where to begin, his expression creasing with frustration the longer words evaded him.

"Whatever you want to say or feel like you need to explain, it's okay." I swallowed the pressure rising in my throat. "We broke up ten years ago—we weren't even old enough to vote when we were together. You lived your life and I lived mine. And even though we're pretending to be back together . . . whatever this is between us . . ." My eyebrows furrowed as I was now stricken with the inability to find the right words. "You don't owe me anything. Not even an explanation."

Chase's arms settled on top of the railing, his attention aimed at the horizon. "A woman came out of nowhere last night and announced to the world she was the mother of my child." His jaw set when he saw my reaction. "I owe you an explanation." His chest moved from the exhale that followed. "I owe you everything."

I pinched off a piece of elephant ear and tossed it to the seagull hovering above us. "You owe me everything for what? Agreeing to be your girlfriend for six months in exchange for a million bucks? Or burning our steaks the night I tried cooking dinner before homecoming? Or maybe because I got us both detention for suggesting we skip sixth so we could make out in your truck?"

A sound rumbled in the back of his throat. "*That* was totally worth a week's stint in detention."

"I'm being serious," I said, launching another scrap of dough at the persistent gull.

"So am I."

"Chase—"

"I owe you everything for a million different reasons." His head tipped toward me. "And I'll gladly list every one if you think I'm not being serious."

He must have read the look on my face as one

of skepticism. "One, for you believing in me when no one else on the planet did. Two, for you buying me my first guitar when I couldn't find two nickels to rub together hiding in the couch cushions. Three, when you stayed up all night refreshing my ice pack after my dad took a swing at me." He took a slow breath. "Four, when you let me make the biggest mistake of my life that day I left you, so I could learn the most valuable lesson of my life as a result."

The corners of my eyes stung, but it was from the wind cutting through the sides of my glasses. "What lesson was that?"

His stare seemed to cut right through my glasses. "Having the love of a good woman is priceless."

I shifted. "This coming from the same man who put a price on me pretending to love him?"

"And I'd let you name your price if we could just drop the pretending part."

I turned around, leaning my back into the railing, my eyes drawn to the weathered planks at my feet. "Everything you're saying is beautiful—a future number-one hit—but I really need to know if that woman was telling the truth last night." My tongue worked into my cheek. I couldn't understand why it was so important I knew if Chase had fathered a child with another woman, but it was. It seemed defining—for him, for us, for the future. "Why are you stalling?"

His throat moved. "Because I'm afraid the truth will scare you."

My boot scuffed at the plank below me. "I'm stronger than you think."

"Em." Chase's head turned toward me. "You're the strongest person I know."

I remained quiet, preparing myself for whatever truths he was about to share.

"That woman was lying," he said, no preamble or closing remarks.

It took me a moment to respond. "How do you know?"

He angled toward me. "I know."

"But *how* do you know?" My hands lifted. "Did you already run up a DNA panel on the little tyke and get the results back in record time? Do you have a picture book with the name and location of every woman you've ever slept with?" Words were flooding from my mouth, the volume dialing up with each one. "Did you double-up on contraceptives every single time you screwed someone?" Shoving off the rail, I spun so I was facing him. "How do you know, Chase?"

For all of my emotion, he was the picture of calm. One of his brows was peeking above his sunglasses as though he were waiting to see if I was done or only getting warmed up.

My arms thrust at him. "This is where you supply a response."

He slid off his sunglasses, his eyes grabbing hold of mine. "This is the part that's going to freak you out."

"Why?"

"For a lot of reasons." He stepped closer. "And I'm not sure you'll believe me."

Plucking off my own glasses as well, I asked, "Is it the truth?"

"Yes." He didn't blink.

"Then that's good enough for me. You might have been a dick for leaving, but you never were a liar."

Chase studied the space between us as though he were looking for a way to bridge it. "I know I don't have a baby with that woman, or any woman for that matter, because . . ." His eyes narrowed as he concentrated on his words. "I haven't been with anyone since you."

His answer didn't register at first. I was sure I hadn't heard him right. "You mean you haven't been with anyone since we started hooking up a few weeks ago?"

Chase exhaled, rolling his head a couple of times. "I mean I haven't been with anyone since the day I left you ten years ago."

My hand reached for the rail, steadying myself. "Chase, come on. I'm not dumb."

"It's the truth. You were my first, my only." His gaze cut back to the ocean. "There's only ever been you."

Something was pounding in my head and my chest. I'd heard his words, but they refused to take root. "You're Chase Lawson. You could literally walk into a gas station and find no fewer than three volunteers who would gladly let you have them in the women's bathroom." I blinked as I thought of the droves of young women who threw bras, numbers, and everything in between at him wherever we went.

"Yeah, but . . ." He slid the glasses back into place. "None of them are you."

"Chase." I didn't know what else to say. His name was the only word I could conjure.

"There it is. My explanation." The weathered boards creaked when he shifted. "Did I just destroy whatever chance we might have had to rewrite our ending?"

I wet my lips, not sure what I was going to say when my mouth opened. "I honestly don't know what to think right now. I guess I just don't understand why you'd crawl into bed alone for ten years when there were droves of women who would have been happy to warm it for you."

His hands slid into his pockets as he studied the masses weaving around the pier. Then he looked at me. "You ruined me for anyone else. Being with you . . . anything else with anyone else would have been a disappointment."

The wind was messing with my tear ducts again, so I settled the sunglasses back into position. "I came into this planning on six months of faking it with you. A couple weeks in and we were already blurring the lines by screwing, and now, you're admitting all of this." My shoulders rose. "I don't know what to say."

"You don't have to say anything, remember? I

was the one who had something to get off of my shoulders."

The toe of my boot tapped his. "You're the only person to ever describe ten years of celibacy as something you're afraid to admit to the last woman you were with."

"Yeah. Maybe." He let out a deep breath, shoving off of the railing after a minute. "So what do you want to do? I've got a wallet full of cash so you can play, ride, and eat to your heart's content."

My shoulders relaxed with the change in topic. I needed time for this to all simmer, and Chase knew it.

"It's still early," I said. "You've got time to make an appearance at that golf thing and whatever else Dani had squeezed into the schedule for today."

He'd begun shaking his head halfway through my response. "The day is clear. Wide open. The next place I have to be is the tour bus by eleven tonight so we can make it to San Francisco for tomorrow night's concert."

I hung my mouth open in mock surprise. "You mean you've got the next fourteen hours free to do whatever you want?"

"To do whatever *you* want."

I felt my eyes light up. "How late do you think

this place stays open?" In my head, I was already making my plan of attack. Rides, then food, then games. Repeat.

Chase roped his arm behind my neck, guiding us back into the fray. "Let's close it down."

## 11

"ONLY MY PARENTS KNOW ABOUT THE DEAL WE made. And I might have mentioned it to Jesse," I rattled off in the truck Chase had rented at the airport as we sped down a familiar gravel road. "Everyone else thinks we're really together."

Chase feigned a wounded expression. "And here I've been thinking we really are together." His hand settled above my knee as naturally as if he'd been doing it for years.

"Hey. No professions. No promises." I lifted my finger. "We promised each other one day at a time for six months. Then we can decide where we want to go from there."

His hand slid a little higher. "So if I were to confess to you that I've never wanted anything more than I want you and that I will commit grievous crimes to remain the man who gets to make love to you . . . would that be a profession or a promise? Because it kind of feels like both to me."

He only laughed when I swatted his arm. "Chase, come on. I'm nervous enough about this whole dinner with the entire hometown crew tonight. I'm worried I'm going to say something wrong or you are or the whole thing's going to wind up in disaster."

"Your dad still keeps his guns locked up, right?"

My face pinched together. "Yeah?"

"Good. That gives me a solid twenty-second lead from the time his patience runs out and he decides he's shown enough self-restraint."

He squeezed at my leg when I sighed. "Not helping. How are you not as nervous as I am about this?"

"Because everything is going to be fine." Chase whipped the truck down a gravel street, knowing these backroads as well as I did. "We're having a BBQ at your parents' house and all of our old friends will be there. What's so terrifying about that?"

"The fact that you'll be in attendance," I muttered.

"It'll be fine."

He ignored his phone buzzing in his back pocket. He'd been ignoring it for the last twenty miles. Chase was playing a show in Tulsa tomorrow night, but when everyone heard we'd be in town a day early, the plots for a get-together had been inevitable. My parents had insisted on hosting, and a couple dozen friends would be in attendance. We'd left the crew back in Tulsa, which was no doubt why Chase's phone was blowing up.

Pete had a serious case of separation anxiety, while Dani was probably busting her bun having to reschedule this evening's previously scheduled festivities.

"I could really use a drink." I was bouncing in my seat the closer we got.

Chase's hand secured me to the seat, drifting even higher up my leg. "Then let's get you a drink, woman. Is that shady old dive still up here on the left?"

My head shook. "I can't drink around you."

"Why not?"

"Because of what happened. Because you don't drink anymore." I flicked the water bottle in his console. "Walking into some sleazy bar and doing a couple of shots in front of you is, like, the least supportive thing I could do."

From the corner of my eye, I could tell Chase was staring at me like I was insane. "You can drink whenever, wherever, and however you want around me. Trust me. Waking up after the buzz wore off to find out I'd totaled a minivan belonging to a mom of four put me off the stuff entirely. You could shake a glass full of my favorite brand of whiskey and I'd have no desire to sneak a sip."

Chewing at my lip, I shook my head. "I admire your discipline. I should stop drinking too. Give it up cold turkey." My voice was all high and breathy. "Where did that expression come from, do you suppose? Cold turkey? How weird of a phrase is that?"

Chase hit the brakes, sending the truck squeeling in a cloud of dust. "I've never seen you so worked up."

"That's because I've never brought you home for the second time after the disaster the first time ended in."

He twisted in his seat toward me. "You need to relax, Em."

"I can't."

He leaned in, his eyes darkening when they

washed down the summer dress I was wearing. "I can make you."

A puff of air burst from my mouth. "A pharmacy of highly controlled substances couldn't at this point. What makes you think you can?"

His hand slid beneath the hem of my dress. "Carnal knowledge." He leaned in, his mouth grazing my collarbone right before his teeth nipped at the delicate skin. "Of a very particular sensitive spot on your body." When his hand reached the apex of my legs, his knuckles skimmed down my panties. "All I need is two minutes and a willing attitude."

My back tensed when his pinkie tucked inside my panties, a throaty growl coming from him when he felt my "willingness."

"Chase." I glanced at the side-view mirror when he unbuckled, his hand tugging my panties down my hips. "A car could be coming."

He leaned over my lap, his head dipping under my dress as he shoved my legs apart. "I don't give a fuck." He sucked me into his mouth in a way that had me grabbing the headrest behind me as though I were trying to tear it off. "The only thing I'm worried about coming right now is you."

WHEN WE MADE OUR APPEARANCE AT MY PARENTS'
that afternoon, I was relaxed. Flustered and
fidgeting with the hem of my dress to make sure it
was back where it was supposed to be, but as calm
as could be expected given the circumstances.

Even as a fifteen-year-old girl, convincing my
family and friends that Lloyd Lawson's son had
more to offer than the shadow his father cast in
town had been difficult. My friends had warmed
up to Chase first, my parents a while after, but
after he'd bailed, all bets were off. I really wasn't
sure how he'd be received by everyone tonight,
but if Chase was at all concerned, he didn't
show it.

"It looks exactly the same as I remember."
Chase paused outside my door after opening it to
stare at the farm. There was the shadow of a smile
on his face, but it fully manifested when his gaze
traveled to the old porch swing we'd shared our first
kiss on.

"Some things never change."

"Thank god," he replied softly.

I heard a din of voices coming from behind the
house, where my parents hosted the majority of the
fair weather get-togethers. A person could watch
the sunset light up a field of wheat from the perch

of a picnic bench, then move on to dancing on an earthen floor beneath a shelter of white lights.

"Ready?" I asked him as we rounded the side of the house.

"I've got my bullet-proof vest in place and my best self-deprecating lines in a queue. I'm set."

When he took my hand, the tension in my shoulders melted. There was something so simple about my hand inside of Chase's, it ushered away the complexities of life.

The buzz of voices dropped to silence when we came into view around back. What felt like a hundred sets of eyes zeroed in on us, the thoughts behind those stares on display for anyone to read.

Mom was the first one to break through the crust of surprise, holding out her arms as she approached. My throat tightened when I saw her, a happy sob escaping when she gathered me into her arms. Twenty-eight years old, and my mom's hug could still fix just about anything.

"Goodness gracious, I missed you." She kissed my temple, patting my back. "Phone calls and texts just aren't the same as a good old-fashioned hug."

Just over her shoulder, I could make out Dad making his way toward us. Slowly. Each step closer had a direct effect on the tension in his jawline.

When Dad ended up in front of us, he gathered me up as Mom had, hugging me as though it had been a lifetime instead of a couple of months. When he let go, he was more relaxed, able to look at Chase without a gleam that suggested he wanted to behead him.

"Chase." Dad tipped his head in acknowledgment.

"Mr. North," Chase replied. "Thanks for having me here. I know how you must feel about me."

Dad moved closer. "I lost my respect for you ten years ago when you left the way you did. But I swear to god if you hurt her this time, I will not exercise the same self-control I showed back then."

Chase held out his hand. "I hurt her, and I'll hand you the shotgun."

Dad looped his thumbs behind his belt buckle, sniffing. "Heard about that woman who claimed to be the mother of your baby. How did you manage to get that brouhaha to go away so quickly?"

Beside Chase, I tensed. I should have known my dad would lead with the heavy artillery first.

"Because it wasn't true," Chase replied, his face the picture of calm. "I'd never met the woman before in my life and I sure as hell hadn't made a baby with her." Chase tipped his head at my mom. "Pardon my language, Mrs. North."

"You have some kind of DNA test to confirm it? The little tyke didn't have your eyes? What made you so sure it wasn't your kid?" Dad pressed, the wrinkles along his forehead setting deeper.

"The baby isn't mine." Chase's hand came to rest on my lower back, knowing how sensitive I was about the issue. Even after his explanation and being on the diminishing end of the media craze, I still bore a sore spot where other women were concerned. There might not have been any others in the intimate sense, but there were literally tens of thousands willing to sell their souls for a night with Chase Lawson. It hadn't bothered me in high school because those girls I knew and could chase away if need be, but how did a person contend with an entire planet of competitors?

I couldn't, so I either had to accept it or step aside.

"If the kid isn't yours, why did I hear you set up some kind of trust for its college education?" Dad shook his head when Mom started to interject. "Why does a person do that if they're not somehow responsible for that little life?"

"I guess I do." Chase's big shoulders moved

beneath his shirt. "The way I see it, if that woman is claiming I'm the father of her baby, it must mean the real daddy isn't in the picture. I figured that kid could use every leg up he could get, so that's why I set up the trust. I take care of my responsibilities, Mr. North. And I also do the responsible thing."

I relaxed, giving Chase a small smile. I hadn't understood at first why he'd decided to set aside college money for a baby that wasn't his—it seemed as though it would only give credit to the woman's claims—but I got it now. He'd done the right thing.

"And what if more woman come forward claiming to be carrying your babies? You gonna bankroll every one of them too?" Dad's voice wasn't as gruff as it had been, though he was still staring at Chase like he was fantasizing about squashing him under the heel of his favorite boots.

"Don't know. I can't predict the future. All I know was that to that one kid, I was able to make a difference." Chase's mouth twitched at one corner. "But if this keeps happening, I might have to consider dropping some hints to the media that I'm gay. I know some of the tabloids already have their suspicions, so it shouldn't take too much convincing."

When I crossed my arms and gave him a look,

all he did was pinch my backside. Lucky for him, my daddy didn't see and I didn't flinch.

"My life would be a hell of a lot easier if you were gay, son." Dad shook his head, holding out his hand.

Like me, Chase gaped at my father's extended hand for a few minutes before realizing what it meant. My dad had never seen Chase fit to shake hands with before.

Mom watched with the same disbelief I was as the two shook hands, though I didn't miss the way both of their grips edged into the excessive zone.

"You kids better go say hi to everyone else. They've been dying to see you." When Chase's forehead creased, Dad clapped my shoulder. "Dying to see *her*."

"Don't worry. I'll protect you," I said to him as we started toward the hub of the party.

"Good to know your friends don't hold onto a grudge," he said with sarcasm.

"They used to be your friends too." I gave him an innocent smile. "Until you committed a treasonous act on one of their own and shall now forever be shunned."

"Hey, Lawson!" one of the guys circled around the horseshoe pit hollered. "Grab a plate and a brew and get your famous ass over here. We've gotta see if you can still play horseshoes or if all that pampering has made you soft."

After waving at the guys, Chase turned to me with a smirk.

I smiled. "Holding a long-term grudge for a guy is like forty-eight hours. Just you wait. The girls will freeze you out."

Chase stuffed his hands in his pockets, grinning at me as he moved backward. "Maybe *some* of us have matured. Maybe some of us realize people can change and even when we do screw up, it's part of life."

My hand settled on my hip. "Seriously, if someone screwed me over and came at me with 'it's part of life,' they would not be walking away with all of their teeth in place."

Chase tapped his temple. "Noted." Then he turned and jogged toward the horseshoe pit, where he was greeted by the guys like he'd never left.

"Just so you know, I threatened Rob with microwave dinners for the next month if he didn't give Chase the cold shoulder for at least the first half of this thing." Brooke sighed as she waved at the guys laughing and dividing into teams. "I guess my cooking still really sucks."

"Or maybe he really loves microwave meals?" I suggested, although it wasn't a secret that Brooke was prone to setting toast on fire.

"Get over here." She weaved her arm through mine to steer me toward the girls staggered around the tables, dishing up their kids' plates or keeping them from putting dirt into their mouths.

"How are you?" Brooke asked, though not the typical way a person asks that question. Hiding between her words was the request for the entire thesis, complete with annotations.

"Things have been really good," I said, reminding myself that my friends didn't know about Chase's and my agreement. "Weird, kind of, and sometimes confusing . . . but good."

Jesse and Sophia were creeping their way into earshot, still watching their little ones like hawks.

"Weird. Confusing. Good." Brooke blinked at me, waiting for a drawn-out explanation.

"It's Chase and me. Back together after the mess we left things in." I smiled my thanks when Jesse handed me a cold bottle of beer. "It's not going to be a rosy picnic. It never was."

"Yeah, but what in the world possessed you to get back with him after what he did to you?" Sophia asked, pointing her beer in Chase's direction. "I mean, yeah, he's a handsome son of a bitch and he's probably got more money than a Saudi prince, but you're not shallow like that. Right?" Sophia shifted as her face fell. "Please don't tell me you're shallow."

"He's not *that* rich or good-looking." As I took a drink of my beer, three sets of eyes narrowed on me. "Okay, fine, he is on both counts, but that's not why we're back together."

"Then why? Because the night of the reunion, your Loathing Meter was at record-breaking levels where Chase was concerned. And then I find out a few days later you guys are back together and you're going on tour with him." Sophia stepped closer, inspecting me as though she were looking for signs of alien abduction. Or possible demon possession.

"I don't know. It just happened. We talked that night and that was that."

"You *talked*?" Brooke said. "That must have been one earth-shattering, mind-blowing talk."

I swatted her arm. "Hate to disappoint that dirty mind of yours, but conversation is all we made that night."

"And what? He talked you into getting back

together?" Brooke asked. "You straight up hated him, Em."

"He talked me into giving him a second chance. And I didn't hate him. I hated what happened."

Brooke gestured toward the guys. "It was all his fault what happened."

"A young boy made a mistake." I shrugged.

"Yeah, maybe . . . but I'm more concerned about the grown woman making her own." Brooke's arm wound around my waist before she tipped her head against mine. "Just be careful, 'kay? I don't want to see you hurt like that again."

"Don't worry." My gaze fell upon Chase, and that familiar tightness gripped my chest. "I'm taking it one day at a time," I said to my friends, though it was more a promise to myself.

Three months and eight days left.

## 12

"Halfway through." Mom handed me one of the homemade pies to set out for dessert. "You seem like you're holding up well." She eyed me from the side as she pulled a big tub of vanilla bean ice cream from the freezer.

"I am," I said, winding out of the kitchen.

"And things between you two seem civil." Mom followed me after grabbing an ice cream scoop.

"Yep."

My tone must have alerted her first, but when she came up beside me, studying my face, she exhaled. "Emma Grace North."

I ducked out through the slider before she could lock me inside the house and interrogate me.

When she caught up with me, I said, "It's nothing."

"That blush on your face implies otherwise."

My steps slowed as we approached the party. It was dark now, the strung lights casting a soft glow on the festivities. Dad had lit a fire in the pit and everyone seemed to be congregating around it, except for one figure sticking to the shadows. Chase had Brooke's littlest settled against his chest and was gently bouncing as he walked, trying to soothe the wailing baby. I'd never seen him holding a baby before . . . and it was probably a good thing I hadn't.

My lungs clocked out while my ovaries went on high alert.

"Sweetie, listen, I know he was young when he left and I know nobody's perfect." Mom set the bucket of ice cream on the table with the rest of the pies. "But I also know some things are better left in the past." She gave my wrist a soft squeeze, tipping her head in Chase's direction. "History lessons are for learning, not reliving."

I tried to tear my eyes from him, but it was a physical impossibility. "I promised him six months. That's all."

Mom took the pie from me and set it down.

"Don't forget to remind yourself of that the next time you get that look in your eyes when you see him." She shifted in front of me, her wrinkles set deeper than usual.

Clearing my throat, I shook off my temporary paralysis. "What look?"

Mom turned to slice the pies. "The one that says you've already named all six kids you're imagining having of his."

"Mom—"

"Here. I'm guessing apple pie's still his favorite." She held out a plate of freshly sliced pie for me to take.

I nodded and scooped some ice cream over the pie. "It is."

Mom moved on to the next plate. "Some things don't change."

I scampered away before she could go into any detail. Of course Mom had figured it out, but she had the sense not to tell Dad. If he so much as suspected Chase and I were kinda back together for real he'd have been hauled off in a police cruiser hours ago.

"Pie?" I said quietly as I came up behind him, not about to wake the baby now that it wasn't screaming anymore.

Chase circled around, still bouncing as he patted the baby's back. He smiled when he saw me.

"It's apple," I said, holding up the plate. "Sorry we don't have crustless kale paste pie."

Chase lifted his finger before heading toward a stroller. He somehow managed to get the baby from his chest to the stroller without waking her, then he tucked a light blanket around her. Motioning over at Rob before pointing at the stroller and making a sleeping face, he strolled my way.

"Your charades game is on point," I said, holding out the plate.

"Only surpassed by my baby whispering game." He dove into the pie the instant he took it from me.

"Yeah, I noticed that. Since when did you become such a pro with babies?"

He finished his bite before replying. "I get a lot of babies dropped, thrown, and pushed into my arms. Necessity is the quickest teacher." He held the next bite up for me.

I made the same kind of face he was after taking a bite. "My mom makes a mean apple pie."

"The best," he said before downing another massive bite.

"It seems like the night's gone rather well for you. Welcomed back into the traitorous group with open arms, horseshoe victor, and champion of babies." I caught my hand as it was moving to his chest, tying it behind my back with the other one.

"It's been an amazing night." The lights in his eyes flickered.

Lifting onto my tiptoes, I whispered, "You want to get out of here?"

He set the plate on the closest table. "Do you think they'll miss us?"

"No," I answered too quickly. "Maybe. But by the time they do, we'll be long gone."

There was a shadow of debate in his expression.

"Come on. I want to show you something."

He followed me, his mouth sliding into an uneven line. "My favorite something you could show me?"

I exhaled. "Is sex always on your mind?"

"*You* are always on my mind." He smacked my backside once he caught up, making me flinch. "So yeah, sex is pretty much always on my mind too."

"You're slapping my ass and talking about sex while sneaking off into the dark with me while my dad is fifty yards away. You're walking thin ice, Lawson."

He glanced back at the party still in full swing, the cluster of people gathering around the fire. His shoulders rose. "I'm just following the woman luring me out onto that thin ice with her."

"This way," I said once we were around the side of the house. "Try to keep up."

My legs took off through the field, carrying me as though gravity or speed had no hold over my body. I heard him behind me, thrashing through the tall grass, his laugh tangling with mine. I felt like a kid again, like the summer Chase and his dad had first moved to town and we'd become fast friends after becoming faster enemies. He was as much a part of my life as these fields were, the soil that generations of my ancestors had worked before me.

The old house came into view when we peaked the next hill, and I paused to give us a second to catch our breaths.

Chase was breathing as hard as I was when he shouldered beside me. "I had other plans for this energy than racing through a mile's worth of wheat field."

"Then we better walk the rest of the way." My hand slid into his before we cut through the last bit of field toward the old homestead.

Chase finally noticed what we were moving toward. "This is where we used to play hide-and-seek as kids."

I nodded.

His fingers tightened around mine. "What game did you have in mind to play now as adults?"

I fought my smile. "Monopoly," I said, all matter-of-fact.

He frowned. "Monopoly?"

"I rolled the dice, landed on a square that gave me one million dollars. I'm spending it to restore this place."

Chase regarded the house with different eyes. "And here I thought you were planning on blowing it all on male strippers and cocaine."

"That's my Plan B."

He chuckled as we rolled to a stop at the bottom of the dilapidated staircase heading to the porch. "Seems a little big for one person."

My head twisted in his direction. "The man who lives in a mansion that makes other mansions look like shacks did not just say that."

He drew a zipper across his lips, his eyes amused.

"And for your information, I'm going to turn it into a B&B with a working farm twist." I started up the stairs, keeping to the sides.

Chase followed me, footstep by footstep. "So

people get to pay to help you with chores? That's brilliant."

I shot a glare back at him. "And enjoy their own luxurious bedroom suites, and homemade meals, and fresh cookies every night while they watch the sunset from the back deck. Which I'm planning to have expanded by two hundred square feet at least."

Chase met me with a raised brow when we made it to the front door.

"I'm selling an experience, a reprieve from the noise and hustle of urban life."

"What says reprieve more than scrubbing out water troughs and wrestling hay bales in the dead of summer?" When I went to shove his chest, his hands wound around my wrists. "I'm messing with you. I think it's a great idea. Knowing you and what you'll put together here, you'll probably have a wait-list a solid year out."

I studied his expression, looking for a crack of sarcasm.

"I'm being serious. I can totally see it," he continued.

Satisfied, I opened the door and led him inside.

Chase gave a low whistle. "You are really going to need every last cent of that million, aren't you?"

"It might need some work, but it's got good bones." When I tapped the newel-post at the bottom of the stairway leading to the second floor, it creaked as it wobbled.

Chase examined the foyer, zeroing in on one of the walls that had several large holes dotting it. "Yeah, *some* work ought to do it."

I positioned myself inside the door, holding up my hand. "Just picture this. A family drives up the rustic, meandering driveway, greeted by the scent of fresh-cut hay and the sounds of the menagerie of farm animals coming from the barn."

Chase moved toward the window I was pointing out. "*What* barn?"

"The one I'm going to have built." I waved off whatever his next question was, continuing to paint my image. "This place has been restored by master artisans who know the importance of honoring tradition at the same time embracing modern advancements. Everything about the entrance is welcoming, inviting." I motioned my arms as if I was inviting guests inside. "I'll be here to greet them and show them to their room, letting them know they're at home. The breakfasts will be hardy, the mattresses exactly the right balance of softness after a day of hard work, and the memories will be priceless."

Chase ducked his head into one of the rooms down the hall. "You'll be in the master bedroom?"

"That will be the master suite. I'll be taking one of the smaller rooms upstairs."

His footsteps creaked as he passed through the house. "Show me."

I made sure he was following my exact footsteps again as we traversed the staircase. "You've been in it." I skipped the next stair. "It's got the really good view to the north."

"Is this the one with the creepy closet that was a really good place to hide in? Or the room with the old light fixture that looked like a deformed mushroom?"

I led the way down the hall once we'd made it to the second floor. "It's the one with the good view."

"Yeah. I don't remember that one."

We passed by a long line of rooms before stopping outside of the one at the end of the hall.

I pushed the door the rest of the way open, breathing a sigh of relief when the door didn't fall off the hinges the way it sounded it might. "It also happens to be the smallest room in the house."

When Chase stepped inside, he did a slow spin. "I thought this was a big closet or something. I didn't realize it was a bedroom."

I bounded toward the window and gently worked up the old blind. "But it's got the best view in the house." I wiggled open the window as far as it would go.

The floor whined as Chase crossed the room toward me. Cool summer air filtered into the room, chasing away the smell of must and making the cobwebs tremble.

"Hey, if you're forced to sleep on a double bed for the rest of your life, at least you've got a window with a view." He stopped beside me, gazing out at the glow of the wheat fields glittering beneath a waxing moon.

"A double bed is more than enough room for me."

"Maybe for *only* you."

I angled toward him. "Implying what?"

"*Implying* there's not going to be any room for anyone else." He gestured at the empty room as though it already held a bed.

"*Assuming* I have plans of there being anyone else," I replied, waving at the same spot.

"*Anticipating* you do, and hinting at the fact that

double beds weren't created with his manly size in mind." His eyes gleamed at me, waiting for me to give him hell for hinting at anything future related where we were concerned.

I flattened my hand against his chest, holding him at an arm's length. "And I'd remind him that he's never let space, size, or time limitations stop him before."

"He'd agree with that statement. And feel it is his responsibility to prove that point."

"You've proven that point hundreds of times." My head tipped at him. "Maybe thousands."

"Make this thousands and one." Chase's eyes moved down me, stopping at a certain spot. "Take off your panties."

His lack of apology or request in his tone was more of a turn-on than it should have been.

My hands slipped beneath my dress, fingers tangling under the sides of my underwear. "Say please."

"If it was a request, I would have worded it that way. But it wasn't." Chase's eyes narrowed when he noticed me stop working off my underwear. "You don't cap an order with a please."

"Damn," I rumbled, giving one last tug that

sent my underwear to my ankles. "Someone's in a mood."

His jaw ground as he stared at the rumple of cotton circling my ankles. "Take off the rest."

"Chase, seriously." Both hands went to my hips instead of working to free me of my dress as he'd instructed. Or *ordered*. "This assertive bullshit doesn't do it for me."

Saying nothing, he closed the distance between us in two long strides, holding my eyes to his. His hand dove under my dress. When I jolted, his other hand plastered to my back, holding me in place, as he pushed two fingers inside me.

This time when I jolted, my body bucked against his, bowing as he moved deeper. "Your mouth is saying one thing"—he sucked my bottom lip into his mouth, nipping it—"and your pussy is telling me something else." Slipping his fingers from me, he lifted them in front of me, all glistening and wet.

A breathy sound slipped from my lips without my consent. The predator inside him rose, reflecting back at me in his pupils.

"Now," he gritted, releasing me all at once before taking a few steps back. "Take off the rest."

My hands moved of their own accord, yanking

the straps down my shoulders and tugging the dress when it fought the challenge of my chest. Chase watched, grabbing himself through his jeans when my chest bounced free of the dress.

Stepping out of my panties and dress at the same time, I lifted my hands. "What do you want me to do next, bossy? The damn Hokey Pokey?"

He rubbed his chin, his eyes a dizzying polish of want and control. "By all means, please do. But when you turn yourself around, make sure it's followed by dropping to your hands and knees."

My thighs squeezed at his words, from the look on his face as he said them. I wasn't sure I'd ever wanted Chase as badly as I did right now. Slipping out of my sandals as I turned around, I stared out the window as I lowered to my knees. I'd spent plenty of hours staring out this window, all types of weather and hours of the day, but *never* like this.

The sound of him approaching caused millions of bumps to rise on my skin. The roughness of his jeans rubbing against my legs had my head swimming. The sound of his zipper lowering sent every muscle contracting.

There was no warning, adjusting, or bracing, there was only one moment he wasn't inside me, and the next, he was. My cry spilled out into the night, scattering across the wheat like a faint breeze.

Chase's fingers tunneled into my hips, drawing me into him until he could claim no more of my body. When he leaned over me, his mouth settled behind my ear. One hand dropped to where our bodies were joined, circling the junction before drawing a wet line up my stomach.

"I can tell how much you don't like me ordering you around." He flicked one of my nipples in a way that made sounds of desire and discomfort fall from my mouth. "How much it bothers you when I tell you to get your ass up in the air and moan my name like a filthy little nympho."

He only had to grind inside me once more to set loose my orgasm. The sheer surprise of it made it that much stronger, my whole body going slack as pleasure raked through me, flooding every nerve ending and muscle fiber.

Chase's arm wound beneath my hips, holding me from collapsing to the floor as he battered into me, finding his own release when my body spasmed at the end of my own.

We remained connected as we fought to catch our breaths, the sweat coating my back cooling in the night air. The remnants of our lovemaking was trickling down my thighs, pooling onto the weathered boards below us. My knees and hands felt rubbed raw, the rest of me in some state of sore or weak, but I'd never felt more alive than I did right then.

Having just made love, having just *fucked*, inside the room that would one day be mine if all went according to plan, gazing out at the land I loved.

"Fuck me." Chase breathed raggedly, going from looking out the window to down at me. "This room really does come with the best view."

## 13

———

"Two nights. No promises. No professions." Chase's arm tightened around me. "Or something like that."

"I can actually tell when you're mocking me," I replied, waiting in the limo with him while his security cleared the sidewalk. "And it worked, didn't it? Taking it one day at a time, staying in the present instead of looking to the future or getting stuck in the past?"

"It did work." Chase stepped outside once we had the okay, holding out his hand for me as I climbed out after him. "But tomorrow night's the last leg of the tour. Eventually, we're going to have to bridge the topic of the future."

My finger flattened against his lips as we

whisked across the dark sidewalk. "There is no future. Only this very moment."

Chase held out his fist to bump Pete's as we passed him holding the unmarked door open for us. "For a country girl, you make a convincing Buddhist monk."

"I'm serious though. No future talk or else."

His eyes flashed. "Or else what?"

"*Or else* should be all the threat that's required. Let your imagination fill in the rest." The sound of my heels connecting with the concrete echoed through the long hallway. "Why are we taking the back way into this place, by the way? It's not like your presence is going to remain a mystery for long."

His shoulders moved beneath his close-fitting shirt. "Yeah, but it might remain a mystery for an extra five minutes it wouldn't have if we'd strolled through the main doors."

The sound of music and people was already hitting me from halfway down the hall. I could almost feel the beat of the drum vibrating the floor. "And what possessed you to visit one of Nashville's biggest honky-tonks the night before you play a sold-out home crowd?"

Chase smiled. "Tradition."

"Tradition?"

"At the end of every tour, we come here as a celebration that we survived. It's my way of thanking the staff for working so hard."

We paused at the next door, waiting for the okay from the guard stationed there. From the sound of things, the place was packed and the acoustics were made to amplify.

"You bring your people to a packed, noisy honky-tonk as a way to show your undying thanks?" I blinked at him.

One corner of his mouth pulled up. "Yeah?"

I sighed. "I hope you at least pick up the tab."

"Of course." He rubbed his mouth. "Up to two drinks."

Pete slid in front of us and moved through the door first, leading us into the joint. We were spit out into some quiet-ish corner of the club, the mass of people and noise coming from across the room.

I'd been to plenty of country bars, but none like this. Country in Nashville was different than country in Tulsa. Or anywhere else for that matter, I guessed. Here, the glitz meter was off the charts. People were still sporting boots and belt buckles, but they were so shiny they could have been picked up by a satellite. Even the music being played by the band up front was a little different. Country, but right where it blurred the lines with rock n' roll.

"This place is insane." I had to shout at Chase as Pete continued to weave us through a maze of tables.

"It's early. And a weeknight." Chase kept his head slightly tipped down, just enough to keep any casual onlookers from potentially recognizing him.

"I don't want to imagine." I glanced at the packed dance floor, the bar area spilling over with bodies. "You like this place?"

He scooted me closer to him when we wove through the crowd circled around a long line of pool tables. "The staff does."

"You're going to get mobbed if you're recognized." I eyed the table of women we were passing.

A sound rumbled in Pete's gut. "Not when I'm around."

"That's why I've got the best security in show business." Chase thumped Pete's chest and it practically sounded like a gong. "And we always rent a private VIP room to keep the mobs from mobbing." He slid aside a thick curtain, gesturing me inside the hidden room.

"Okay, this is *not* a honky-tonk, Chase Lawson, and you know it." I gaped at the private room that dripped extravagance. And yeah, there might have been a country motif . . . if a person could see past the crystal wall sconces and studded leather furniture.

"Maybe to a couple of Oklahoma kids, but it is for a bunch of people from Nashville." Chase waved at everyone in the room.

They'd started clapping when he appeared. For a few dozen people, they could make one hell of a raucous.

His drummer, Lane, handed him a bottle of sparkling water and me my favorite kind of beer. "Speech!"

Chase tried waving off the chant that followed, but he gave in when he must have realized that they weren't going to give up. "It seems by now you all should be tired of hearing me run my mouth, so I'll keep it short and sweet." He held up his sparkling water as he cut into the center of the room. "I'm one person who knows his way around a guitar and can carry a tune most days of the week. It's because of you I am where I am today. Cheers to your skills at fooling America into thinking I'm kinda a big deal."

A parade of drinks launched into the air

followed by a roar of an echo, bottles clinking glasses, cans cracking cups.

"Now go open your presents already!" Chase pointed at a table in the back, where rows of silver gift bags were propped.

A mad dash nearly ensued. Pete broke character by behaving more like a preschooler on his birthday than a fully-grown man who knocked skulls for a living.

Chase headed my way and touched his bottle to mine. "Thank you for believing in me. Always."

"You made it." I took a sip of my beer, motioning between him and the room. "Not sure you'd feel the same gratitude if you were still submitting samples and playing originals on sidewalk corners."

He brushed a strand of hair back from my face. "I would."

"We'll never know."

"You might not. But I do," he replied.

A chorus of shrieks and whoops grew from the table as members of his staff tore into their bags. I wasn't sure I'd seen so many adults behave like they'd won the lottery at the same time.

"What in the world's in those bags? A one-way ticket to Santa's workshop?" My mouth fell open when I saw Dani actually jumping as she clutched some paper certificate in her hands.

Chase winked at his staff hollering gratitude and disbelief in equal measure. "Bonus checks," he answered me, grinning as he watched everyone's reactions. "And I always send everyone and their family on a nice vacation the day after the tour ends."

"Like they all go to Hawaii or the Caribbean?" I asked, watching Pete chatter excitedly to someone on his phone.

"We all spent the last six months together. I figure the last thing anyone wants to do is spend any more time together." Chase took my hand and led me to a leather couch, the kind that looked worn but had probably cost thousands of dollars to create the effect. "They go by themselves or with their families."

"How do you pick where to send them?" I asked.

Chase looked surprised by my question. "I *know* them. They might work for me, but they're my friends too."

My eyebrows drew together as he pulled me into his lap on the couch. "So what? You have them

fill out a survey listing their top ten vacation desti-
nations?"

"They talk. I listen." He wound both arms around
my waist. "Pete casually mentions on a rainy night in
Denver that he wishes he were in Rio again. Or I catch
Dani perusing a New Zealand travel book over coffee
in the morning." From out of nowhere, a silver bag
appeared in front of me. "Or I remember some girl
from my childhood rattling my ear off about some trip
she'd love to take one day when she was all grown up."

My breath caught. Taking the bag from him, I
reached inside, telling myself not to cry no matter
what I pulled out. In my hands was a voucher from
a travel agent. In the "For" line was scratched in
familiar handwriting, *All-Expense Paid Trip to Iceland.*

My eyes stung as I reread the line. How had he
remembered when I'd forgotten?

"You wanted to see the northern lights, glaciers,
and hot springs. You wanted to go caving and try
Skyr and see if people really ate seabirds," Chase
listed, while I wiped my eyes to make sure they
weren't leaking.

"I'm not one of your employees. We made our
own kind of agreement I'm getting more than
compensated for." I brushed the word Iceland with

my thumb, feeling all my childhood dreams and whims come spilling back.

"Yeah, well, that part of the agreement's in there too." Chase flicked the gift bag. "Don't lose it. I had to go to five different banks to get that many twenties."

I reached back inside, finding a check instead of a mountain of bills. The number of zeros following the one took my breath away. At the same time, my stomach sunk. "I agreed to six months," I said, sticking the check back in the bag. "I haven't fulfilled my end of the bargain yet."

"So it's a day early. Don't cash it until tomorrow if it makes you feel better."

I placed the travel voucher into the bag as well before setting it on the sofa. "I don't know what to say. Part of me knows I shouldn't accept the trip . . . but I really, *really* want to go." Chase laughed at the conflicted look on my face. "And another part of me knows a million dollars in exchange for the past six months is totally unfair."

He rubbed at the crease between my eyebrows. "You're right, because I would have given every last dollar in exchange for the past six months."

My hand covered his where they were still cinched around my stomach. They were strong hands, rough, calloused from playing guitar, but I preferred the feel of them against my skin over the softest cashmere. "It *has* been pretty great."

"Exactly. So take your seven figures knowing I got the better end of the deal."

Silence found us then. The room was anything but, however a bloated quiet grew from the unsaid. What came after? What next? He'd asked for six months. I'd agreed to six. We'd made no promises to each other for the future, no grand professions that hinted at where, if anywhere, this path would lead us after tomorrow night.

I shouldn't have felt so uneasy about it—I'd been the one to create those boundaries to protect myself. To safeguard whatever was left of my heart post-Chase Lawson.

"Why was it so important I join you on this tour anyway?" I shattered the silence, twisting to look at him. "You made it seem like it would be such a game-changer to your public image if you and your high school girlfriend reunited . . . but you did a better job of that on your own by not drinking and staying out of trouble. I really have no idea what I did to help you." I rubbed my temple. That night at the reunion, he'd made it sound so simple, so straightforward, but looking back, I thought I had been too dumbfounded by the whole offer to consider how my presence could play such a big role in shining him up in the public eye.

If anything, I might have polished up the impression that Chase Lawson could stay in a committed relationship with a mere mortal instead of a Perfect Ten as I guessed the public pictured him with. But that was only a fraction of a fraction of an image—Chase had cleaned up the rest all on his own.

He took a minute to consider his reply before tangling his fingers through mine. "'From Bad Boy to Golden Boy.' 'The Comeback of Our Generation.' 'Reputations are Earned, Not Made.' 'First Love Replay,'" he said slowly, reciting some of the bigger headlines that had risen to the top of the media circus. "I could keep going all night, but the point I'm trying to prove is that it worked, Em. *You* worked."

"None of those sound bites were about me. They're about you, Chase. *You* did it. All by yourself. You didn't need me to keep you sober or improve your public image or hell, tell you when you need to change into a fresh shirt."

The look on his face suggested I'd somehow wounded him. Or maybe astonished him. "Em," he breathed, his eyes drowning in an emotion I didn't have a name for. "I need you for *everything.*"

Something buried deep in my chest went soft. "You've got people who take care of every component of your life, from planning your meals to changing your sheets to planning your schedule down to the last minute. There's no room for whatever else you think you might need from me in there."

A puff of air burst from his nose as he gaped at me in utter disbelief. "Every person on this planet needs a reason to get up in the morning, and *you*, you are that for me." One of his hands molded into the bend of my neck. "You're my reason, Em."

My lips met his before I'd consciously reacted to his words. I knew I needed to protect myself where Chase was concerned, but these were the last two nights we had. I was going to live them like they were the last two of the planet's existence.

"I want to dance with you." His words vibrated against my lips as he rose from the couch, setting my feet on the floor in front of him.

"You're going to get attacked if you go out there," I warned when he led me out of the room.

"Worth it."

"You might not feel the same if a herd of

crazed females dismembers you a piece at a time, painting themselves in your blood."

"We all gotta go sometime, Em, and dancing with you is second on my list when it comes to preferred ways to expire."

Pete noticed my arm flailing back at him, and he grabbed the other Man in Black before they came charging after us.

"Dare I ask what's number one?" I asked, breathing a sigh of relief when Pete and Nate broke in front of Chase right before he stepped out of the room.

"You can ask. But if you don't know, I haven't done my job of proving my priorities to you. Let me rectify that. Right after this. In my bed. Let me really bring it home. I've got until six forty-five tomorrow night to enlighten you."

When we carved through the main part of the club, he pulled me up beside him, tucking his arms and chest around me like he was some kind of human shield. Of course, the four giant-sized guards moving with us were their own kind of impenetrable shield.

"Your concert's at seven," I reminded him.

He grinned at me. "Plenty of time to spare."

Any other conversation in words would have to

wait, because there was no more hiding the fact that Chase Lawson was there. Shouts and shrieks, all crying his name, grew until it felt like the floor was vibrating from the noise. Phones rose by the hundreds, followed by thousands of flashes firing until even when I blinked, I could still see little white balls seared onto the back of my eyelids.

"Mr. Lawson, we should get you back to the private room." Pete's deep voice managed to cut through the noise.

"I second that," I shouted, but I didn't think anyone heard.

Chase shook his head, continuing to guide me to the crowded dance floor, while I clung to him, trying not to flinch each time some hand cut through the Muscle Wall and brushed against me, fingers grappling at Chase. We were surrounded by adults behaving as though one touch would instantly heal their dying child. People who had made enough wise choices in their life to get them to this point without dying were currently losing their minds because some guy they had on their iPod was sharing the same breathing space.

Life was weird.

People were weirder.

The four guards turned to face the crowd,

forming a tight circle around us, when we finally made it to the dance floor, semi-unscathed.

The band up front didn't miss the commotion, and they stopped playing the song they had been before breaking into a slower melody. It was an old country classic, the kind I'd caught my parents dancing to in the kitchen when they thought I'd gone to bed. The kind Chase and I had made out to in the bed of his truck on sticky summer nights, barefoot and sunburnt.

Chase didn't say anything. He just tucked me to him, holding me close as our bodies remembered how to move together like this. My hands slid up his chest, nestling around the caps of his shoulders. My eyes cut to the spot my pinkie had just passed over.

Chase's shoulder lifted when he checked the tear on his shirt with me, as though it were no big deal, a daily occurrence. But then, it was for him. The lunatic fans, the screaming, crying, and cameras. This swirl of chaos was his life, and he'd adapted to it well. Music was his calling, fame the price to pay. Torn shirts and red scratch marks—I noticed with a small gasp—and all the rest.

Privacy, quiet, anonymity would never follow wherever he went. The past six months, we couldn't share a kiss in public without it being documented and blasted into the world for all to see and scrutinize.

Chase's head lowered to mine, his mouth positioning right outside of my ear. "What is it?"

My fingers brushed the marks on his neck before I scanned the crowd. "That I'm going to miss you."

His throat moved as his fingers curled into my lower back, dragging me closer. "I'm right here."

I nodded as I tucked my head to his chest, before he could see the shine setting in my eyes. "I already do."

## 14

"Last night. We made it." Pete deflated a few inches from his exhale, staring at Chase on stage, about to break into his last song of the final concert.

I nudged Pete, knowing I would miss my perch beside him at every concert, watching Chase with the same kind of intent. "Thanks to you."

He didn't argue with me on that. "What are you going to do after this?"

I chewed at my lip. "Go back home."

For the briefest flash, Pete's attention drifted toward me. "And you and Mr. Lawson?"

"I don't know." The words were whispers on my lips.

"Well, no one really does. We all just take a leap

of faith. Sometimes we fall. But we'd never know what it felt like to fly if we didn't take that risk." Somehow, he must have heard my sniffle, because Pete's heavy arm draped around my shoulders for a moment, giving me a brief squeeze. "Life isn't supposed to be easy, Miss North. Don't make your choices with that as a guide."

"Hey, when you retire from this ass-kicking gig, you should go into life coaching."

Pete's body rocked from his silent laugh as Chase's voice filled the stadium with the last few lines.

"I'm not going to miss the ringing in my ears, that's for sure!" I shouted, covering my ears as a roar exploded around us.

Pete winked. "Yes, you will."

I was about to step aside, used to Chase running offstage when the lights dimmed, but that didn't happen. The lights stayed on. Chase remained onstage, behind the microphone, his mouth open as if he was still singing, but no words were coming.

"Is he changing the set up tonight?" I asked Pete.

He grunted. "After working for this guy for eight years, I've stopped trying to keep up with his curveballs."

I stepped toward the stage, waiting, and that was when Chase's head turned, his eyes finding mine. "I need you out here, Emma North."

My stomach dropped at the same time my hand gripped Pete's wrist, hoping someone could tell me what was happening.

The crowd got louder, the whole stadium looking like a disco ball from the way flashes were going off.

My head shook when he waved me out, still grinning at me, fresh from the concert high. "It's the last night, Em."

He was a good thirty feet away from where I stood, but I could see the emotion in his eyes. I could read it.

The second I came into view, the noise amplified, arms jutting into the air as bodies bounced, as though all fifty thousand fans knew something I didn't.

"There she is." Chase gestured at me, pride etched into his face. "There's my girl."

His words made my spine tingle, and for a moment, I forgot I was walking toward him for an unknown reason with thousands of people watching me. It had me checking my outfit to make sure everything was in place and I hadn't wound up mysteriously naked.

When I was within arm's reach, Chase spun his guitar over his back, holding out his hand for me to take. I knew better than to say anything with the microphone so close, but the question in my eyes was easy to read.

Chase's smile spread, the sight of him making my breath strain. "This is it, Em. The last night." His hand ran through his damp hair, his words still ringing through the auditorium. My heart thundered before he reached into his back pocket, pulling something out at the same time he crouched to his knee. His brown eyes melted into mine, the boy I fell in love with reflecting back in the man before me. "Taking it one day at a time led me right here."

When Chase lifted the ring, the roar of the crowd cut out. The flashes. The rumble. All of it. In that moment, there was only Chase and me and that beautiful ring making promises that had yet to be proven and were not guaranteed.

His forehead creased. "All I want is you."

Emotions flooded me. So many all at once. Sadness in my stomach. Anger in my throat. Uncertainty in my knees. But hope . . . I couldn't find a sliver of it hiding anywhere.

My lips trembled as I tried to speak, but words were next to impossible as, bit by bit, the outside world crept back in. The crowd seemed to have quieted some, as though it were holding its collective breath, waiting for my answer.

"Em." Hope hung in his voice, but it had left his eyes. He knew my answer. I didn't need to say it out loud for him to hear.

Fighting the urge to drop to my knees in front of him and kiss away his sadness, I forced myself to turn and run. To walk away when it felt like the hardest thing I'd ever had to do or ever would. To leave behind a good man because of uncertainty, fear, and ultimately, because I was haunted by the past. I'd regret it; I knew that three steps into the journey.

I saw Pete's face first as I rushed offstage, then Dani's. The expressions on both of them were unlike any I'd seen before—eyebrows knitted together in anguish, mouths parted with shock. After them, I couldn't look at anyone else lingering backstage.

I heard him calling my name before I'd made it far. The sound of his footsteps chasing after me. It only made me run faster.

Flying down the stairs, I rounded into the same hall we'd arrived in, praying the door would magically swing open when I approached. It didn't.

"Emma, please!"

Chase's footsteps echoed louder as I fought with the door. When he stopped behind me, I didn't turn around. If I did, I would lose my resolve.

"I shouldn't have asked you that way, in front of all of those people." His breath was rushed from running, and an unfamiliar tenor hung in his voice. "I got caught up in my excitement. I wasn't thinking that asking you to marry me in front of tens of thousands of people would be the last way you'd want to be asked. I'm sorry—"

My head shook. "That's not it."

"Then what is it?" he asked almost tentatively, as though he was scared to know.

My silence stretched as I tried to put into words what not even my heart fully understood.

"What do you want?" he asked, his presence pressing in on me. "Name it. If I can give it to you, it's yours. Just tell me, what do you want, Em?"

My eyes squeezed shut to keep the tears in. I knew the six months would be difficult, and I'd guessed they wouldn't end on the highest of notes, but I'd thought it would be because I despised him, not because I was—I *had*—fallen for him.

"I don't want this." My arm gestured behind me to everything in that massive arena. "The noise, the people, the rumors. The girls." My throat burned. "I don't want this."

A prolonged exhale came from him. "This is part of who I am now. I come with this."

My fingers tightened around the door handle. "I know."

"This is my life, Em." He sounded so young, so vulnerable.

I wanted to stay—but I had to leave. My eyes closed.

"But it isn't mine," I whispered, pushing the door open at last.

## 15

I'D TRAVELED HALFWAY AROUND THE EARTH, BUT my world was still upside down. The change in scenery, the space, the time—nothing could ease the ache I still felt after leaving him that night.

Focusing on the crunch my boots made as I passed over the snow, I attempted to empty my mind, knowing it was a fruitless task. In the week since I'd arrived in Iceland, I hadn't been able to silence my mind once. Not even for half a minute.

The northern lights were churning in the night sky, neon ribbons dancing with one another. It was the most spectacular natural wonder I'd ever witnessed, but it felt flat without having someone to share the experience with. The beauty of this world —of life—was enhanced with a trusted companion to share them with. And even though I'd walked away from Chase, part of me knew that there would never be another who could fill the void he'd left in my life for the past ten years.

It was the classic conundrum of not being able to live with someone, but being unable to live without them at the same time.

I was almost to the back deck of the little cabin I was staying in outside of Reykjavik when I noticed a figure pacing across the deck. She was bundled up like she was about to set out on an Arctic expedition, donning her signature color.

"What are you doing here?" I called.

Dani jumped as though I'd scared her out of her eight-hundred-fill down parka.

"I thought you were supposed to be in Bora Bora," I continued, joining her on the deck.

"I *was* in Bora Bora, *trying* to relax, but I couldn't. So now I'm here, freezing my eyelashes off, waiting to become dinner for a pack of wolves." Dani scanned the snowy landscape, eyes wide and teeth chattering.

"There are no wolves around here. And if there were, you're more like a snack than a meal." I shot her a wry smile as I unlocked the door. "You want to come inside and warm up? I'm guessing you didn't come all this way for the snow and night sky."

Dani rubbed her arms. "I like sand, sunny skies, and warmth. Emphasis on the warmth."

I smiled as I swung the door open for her. I was used to harsh winters and bitter cold, so this didn't bother me one bit, but Dani had been born and raised and still resided in Southern California, where winter was the season in which one put on a sweater because temperatures dared approach the fifty-degree mark.

"Why are you here?" I asked again, kicking the snow off of my boots before coming inside the cabin.

She didn't peel off any of her layers, or even remove her hood, as she inspected the rustic cabin. "It's not obvious?"

I moved toward the kitchen to boil a kettle of water for some tea, hoping that having something to focus on would ease the sting this conversation was bound to create. "He sent you."

"No, of course he didn't send me." Dani huffed, still rubbing at her arms. "But I am here for him."

"Chase doesn't know you're here?" Saying his name made my stomach twinge.

"He wouldn't have let me come if he did."

When I held up a couple of tea options, Dani pointed at the herbal selection. After situating the teabags in their mugs, I went to the hearth to place a few more logs on the fire.

Dani remained quiet, which I wasn't used to. When and if she had something to say before, she'd come right out and said it, no filter, no hesitation. It was both what I admired and disliked about her.

Stoking the coals with a poker, I broke the silence. "You came a really long way to say whatever you came here for. So what was so important you left sun, sand, and warmth for pretty much the total opposite?"

Settling onto the edge of the sofa in front of the fireplace, Dani slid off her hood. She had on a thick wool hat beneath it though, and what looked to be earmuffs below that. I threw another log on the fire.

"There was a reason I didn't like you," she said, looking me straight in the eyes.

"Because I breathed?"

Her hand thrust in my direction. "Because I knew this would happen."

My forehead creased as I glanced around. "That I'd wind up in Iceland?"

Dani looked like she was trying really hard not to roll her eyes. "That you'd hurt him."

My instinct was to argue that she had it wrong, that it was the other way around, but I knew the truth. I *had* hurt him, and in so doing, I'd hurt myself.

The teakettle whistled, forcing some kind of response from me. "He asked me to marry him in front of a stadium of fans when our whole arrangement was fake." I wove past her on my way to the kitchen.

I heard her twist in her seat thanks to the layers of outerwear she was donning. "Nothing about that six months was fake. Other than the arrangement." Dani's voice was as calm as I'd ever heard it. "Go figure. The fake arrangement ended up being fake."

I had to peel off my jacket before I poured the water. This place was fast becoming a sauna, more from the words coming from the petite woman wearing her weight in winter gear than from the roaring fire. "You never liked me, so I'm trying to figure out why you're here talking like you're trying to convince me to get back together with him."

"I might not have liked you because of what I was afraid would happen, and I might not like you very much right now either because of what I predicted did happen." Dani rose from the sofa.

"But I like him more than I dislike you, and you make him happy."

My eyes closed as I struggled to find the right words. "I won't—I'm not—the only woman who could make him happy."

One of her manicured eyebrows edged into her stocking cap. "Just like he's not the only man who can make you happy?"

My tongue worked into my cheek. "Dani . . . he hurt me. He left me."

She shorted. "Here's a guarantee—he's going to hurt you again. That's life. That's *love*. We're humans and, by definition, flawed. He's going to hurt you. And you're going to hurt him. Expect it. Plan on it. But what I've witnessed between you two over the past six months is that your love is bigger than all of that." Dani peeled off her gloves, one finger at a time, staring at me. "And he might have left you as some dumb eighteen-year-old kid, but you left him as a full-grown woman with enough life experience under her belt to know better."

"So what? My leaving him was worse?" I slid her cup of tea across the counter, my hands still shaking. "Is that the big thing you flew here to tell me?"

Dani rolled her eyes, glancing at the messy pile

of sketches I'd drawn for the old farmhouse back home. "I flew here to tell you that you just walked away from the best thing in your life."

The knife in my stomach twisted. "No, the best thing in my life walked away from me a decade ago."

"He still loves you." Dani blew at the steam billowing from her cup. "He *never* stopped loving you."

"Love isn't enough." My eyes dropped as I sniffed.

Dani plowed through my personal bubble, her face so close to mine our noses were nearly touching. "No," she said, eyes narrowing, "it's *everything*."

## 16

I'D BEEN STARING AT THE SAME SPOT FOR WHAT felt like hours. The empty patch of wall directly above the fireplace, where something most definitely needed to be displayed, but it couldn't be just anything. It had to have a level of significance, a piece that tied together the whole theme of this place. The fireplace was the heart of any home in my opinion, a place where bodies gathered around the warmth and light of a good fire, where troubles could be turned to ashes and dreams could ignite.

"Miss North, is there anything else you need done tonight? We finished with the baseboards on the second floor except for the last couple of rooms at the end of the hall. Figured we could finish that up tomorrow before we start building the bookcases in the library."

I forced my focus away from the spot above the fireplace. "You've done more than enough for one day." I smiled at two of the many contractors I'd hired to refinish the old farmhouse. "Thanks for everything."

I waved as they turned to leave, flipping off lights behind them. I calculated in my head how many more weeks we had left before completion. Everything had gone slower than I'd anticipated, and slower than my general contractor had estimated, but that was the way of construction. You couldn't build anything to stand the test of time and weather the storms of life quickly. It took time. And patience.

A couple of months had passed since my trip to Iceland, and despite Dani's last-ditch effort to get me to see reason and return to him, I hadn't. Maybe because I was right. Maybe because I was afraid I'd been wrong. Maybe because I was afraid he wouldn't want me back. There were a lot of uncertainties in my life where Chase was concerned.

Most of all, how I was going to live my life without him.

"I love what you've done with the place." An unexpected voice echoed through the large room.

A smile worked at my lips as I rummaged through my large toolbox, trying not to show my surprise. "It's a work in progress."

"All great things are." His footsteps reverberated closer.

"So I've been told." I took a slow breath before turning to look at him. It had been months since I'd last seen him, though the image of Chase had never left my mind. "Don't you have a new album to be recording?"

His shoulders moved beneath his white shirt, practically glowing from the moonlight draining in through the windows. "That was the plan," he said, staring at me in such a way that made my muscles turn to jelly. "Until you."

"Until me?"

He nodded. "My plans center around you now."

"We haven't seen each other in three months."

"It took me some time to put all of these plans centered around you in place." Lights danced in his eyes as he kept moving closer. "It doesn't happen overnight, you know?"

"I'm not sure I do know. In fact, I'm still trying

to figure out what you're doing here when you're supposed to be in Nashville, making the new album that your publicity team promised the fans this summer." I closed the lid on the toolbox, too flummoxed to distinguish between a wrench and a hammer at this point.

"I'm leaving all of that behind me, Em."

I ignored the way my spine tingled when he said my name. "All of what behind you?"

"My career."

I blinked, confusion thickening. "What do you mean?"

"I'm retiring from my life as Chase Lawson, country singer and star. I'm hanging up that hat and putting on another." He grinned when his stare fell to my arms, where splatters of paint had dried.

"What new hat have you got in mind? Award-winning actor? Real estate tycoon? Rock n' Roll Hall of Famer?"

He shook his head. "Something less in the public eye. Actually, something not in the public eye at all."

"Should I keep guessing? Or are you going to tell me what this new title of yours might be?"

"Your husband."

His words took a moment to process, my heart

responding one way while my mind rallied the other. One held onto the pain, while the other had long ago let go of it.

"I love you, Em. Always have. Always will. And if it takes me every day of the rest of my life to convince you to be my wife, then that's what I'm damn well doing." His hand ran through his light hair, his eyes expressing the agony in his words. "It's you or no one. I've known that from the first day I met you . . . but it took me this long to work up the nerve to tell you."

This time when the tears threatened to come, I didn't stop them. I'd been damming them back too long, too much, and I needed to release them. "You're really retiring?" My voice squeaked from my throat tightening.

Chase retrieved his phone from his back pocket and pulled something up on the screen. When he flipped it around, I read the headline, "Chase Lawson Retiring at the Height of his Career."

He swiped over a handful of others, all similar in tone, before shrugging. "If it's on the internet, it must be real, right?"

My mouth moved as I struggled to catch up to what was happening. "When I said that life wasn't for me, I didn't mean that I wanted you to give it all up. You worked hard to get where you did. You achieved something most people only dream about."

"I'm not concerned with other people's dreams. Only mine. And when I close my eyes and think about everything I could ever want in life, all I see is you." His hand brushed down my forearm, his shoulders relaxing as he did. "And maybe a few little ones with your smile and my sense of mischief."

"You shouldn't have to choose between me and your career."

"I'll choose between you and anything out there, Em, and it will be you every time. One career is a small thing to give up in exchange."

"One career?" I blinked. "You make it sound like you're leaving behind a part-time position as a fry cook instead of being the most famous musician in country music today."

His fingers tangled with mine. "Where you're concerned, they're the same." When he noticed the tears I was finally letting fall, he tucked me to him, strong arms holding me close. "I left you for all that back then. Now it's time for me to leave it all for you."

My arms wound beneath his arms, circling

behind his back, not sure I'd ever felt anything so solid in my life before the connection Chase and I shared right at that moment. "Compromise? It's an important part of all relationships after all."

His head shook against mine. "Not on this. Don't meet me halfway. Let me come to you."

My answer came in the form of a kiss, though I wasn't sure of its exact reply. All I knew, as his mouth moved against mine, was that I'd finally buried the ghosts of the past, extinguished my fears for the future, and found happiness in the present.

"I think I know the perfect thing you can hang in that spot above the fireplace you were staring at earlier." Chase kissed the corner of my mouth, his eyes sliding toward the entryway.

When my gaze followed his, I found his old guitar propped against the wall, the very one I'd purchased for him a lifetime ago when I was the only one he shared his music with. It was scarred from years of use, but it had been well taken care of and still shone like it had that first day he'd picked it up and played his first chord. I supposed all things were like that— some mix of scarred and spotless. The secret was in learning from the wounds and protecting the rest.

"What do you think?" he asked, smiling at the

old guitar with me. "I'm hanging up my guitar for you. Figuratively and literally."

"I think it's found its home."

"I found my home twenty years ago when you offered to share your snack with me on my first day of school because I didn't have one." I felt something cool against one of my fingers, a familiar ring hovering above my fingertip. Chase's throat moved. "I just lost my way, and it took me ten years to find my way back."

My eyes met his. All the answer he needed to find was held within them.

"Welcome home," I whispered as the gold band slid down my finger, accepting the warmth of my skin. My mouth was halfway to his when I stopped myself. "Are you sure this is what you want? Despite what you think, you don't have to give up your career for me. You can have both. You can have me and a family and the legacy you create with your career."

Chase hadn't stopped staring at the ring on my finger, images of the future seeming to flash on a reel before him. Then, with the kind of intention that made a person gasp, his eyes locked on mine. Those same eyes I'd seen so much of my life reflected in—the highs, the lows, and everything in between.

"A man's legacy isn't the number of people who know his name," he said, his words warm against my skin. "It's defined by one good woman who knows him and loves him despite it."

**THE END**

## ABOUT THE AUTHOR

Thank you for reading FOOL ME ONCE
by NEW YORK TIMES and USATODAY
bestselling author, Nicole Williams.

Look out for her next book, releasing this spring!

Nicole loves to hear from her readers.
You can connect with her on:

Facebook: Author Nicole Williams
Instagram: author_nicole_williams
Twitter: nwilliamsbooks
Website: authornicolewilliams.com

**ALSO BY NICOLE WILLIAMS**

ALMOST IMPOSSIBLE (Random House)

TRUSTING YOU & OTHER LIES (Random House)

CRASH, CLASH, CRUSH (HarperCollins)

UP IN FLAMES (Simon & Schuster UK)

DATING THE ENEMY

EXES WITH BENEFITS

ROOMMATES WITH BENEFITS

TOUCHING DOWN

STEALING HOME

MISTER WRONG

TORTURED

COLLARED

HATE STORY

THE FABLE OF US

THREE BROTHERS

CROSSING STARS

DAMAGED GOODS

HARD KNOX

GREAT EXPLOITATIONS SAGA

LOST & FOUND SERIES

FINDERS KEEPERS SERIES

THE PATRICK CHRONICLES

THE EDEN TRILOGY

Manufactured by
Amazon.ca
Bolton, ON